RIVALS' ONE-NIGHT RULE

MELANIE MILBURNE

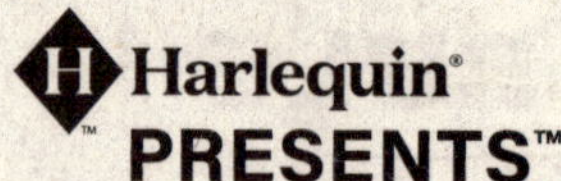

Recycling programs for this product may not exist in your area.

ISBN-13: 978-1-335-61407-0

Rivals' One-Night Rule

For questions and comments about the quality of this book, please contact us at CustomerService@Harlequin.com.

TM and ® are trademarks of Harlequin Enterprises ULC.

Harlequin Enterprises ULC
22 Adelaide St. West, 41st Floor
Toronto, Ontario M5H 4E3, Canada
www.Harlequin.com

HarperCollins Publishers
Macken House, 39/40 Mayor Street Upper,
Dublin 1, D01 C9W8, Ireland
www.HarperCollins.com

Printed in Lithuania

1 2 3 4 5 6 7 8 9 10 LIT 28 27 26 25

Jack eased back from her mouth and looked down at her with lust-glazed eyes.

"Is that as far as this goes?"

Sylvie was so shaken by his kiss, sensually rattled by his caressing mouth, that she found it hard to find her voice. "I...I... Do you want more?" She wanted more. But wasn't that part of Jack's allure to her? He was forbidden fruit and she was tempted beyond her measure of self-control.

"That must be more than obvious."

She was standing so close to him she could feel how much he wanted her. But Sylvie had no time for the fairy tale, only her clients. And yet...there was something missing from her life and it was this—sex. No-strings sex. Fun sex. Exciting, flesh-tingling sex.

Sylvie looked up at him, her heart still pounding from his spine-tingling kiss. "How much more? Are we talking a one-nighter? Because that's all I'd want. A one-off to scratch the itch, so to speak."

Wilde Billionaire Brothers

Brothers Jago, Jack and Jonas were born into the Wilde family's billion-dollar world. But just as quickly as their privileged lives started, their parents' lives tragically ended. So, they began to build their barriers to love as high as the skyscrapers that they owned. But can three exceptional women convince Jago, Jack and Jonas to replace reason with irrational—but oh-so irresistible!—desire...?

Take a walk on the Wilde side with...

Jago and Mollie's story

Fake Engagement Arrangement

Jack and Sylvie's story

Rivals' One-Night Rule

Both available now!

Jonas and Tessa's story

Coming soon!

Melanie Milburne read her first Harlequin novel at the age of seventeen in between studying for her final exams. After completing a master's degree in education, she decided to write a novel, and thus her career as a romance author was born. Melanie is an ambassador for the Australian Childhood Foundation and a keen dog lover and trainer. She enjoys long walks in the Tasmanian bush. In 2015 Melanie won the HOLT Medallion, a prestigious award honoring outstanding literary talent.

Books by Melanie Milburne

Harlequin Presents

The Billion-Dollar Bride Hunt
One Night in My Rival's Bed
Illicit Italian Nights

The Scandalous Campbell Sisters

Shy Innocent in the Spotlight
A Contract for His Runaway Bride

Weddings Worth Billions

Cinderella's Invitation to Greece
Nine Months After That Night
Forbidden Until Their Snowbound Night

Wilde Billionaire Brothers

Fake Engagement Arrangement

Visit the Author Profile page
at Harlequin.com for more titles.

To Grace Matcham, who came into our life at just the right time. You are such a wonderful person who always goes the extra mile for us. It is no wonder Teddy and Louis love you so much. Thank you for taking them for walks when I've not been able to. With much love. xxxxx

A special mention to my previous editor Hannah Rossiter. It was so lovely to work with you over many books. Your support and encouragement during rough patches helped me so much. xxxx

CHAPTER ONE

SYLVIE RATHBONE WOKE to the sound of jackhammers for the fourth time that week. Not the kind of jackhammers inside her head after a big night out with her co-workers, but the construction kind. Next door. Not that she'd had any big or small nights out lately. Her work as a divorce lawyer gave her little opportunity for partying. Or dating. But that was her choice—a dating drought brought on by dealing daily with couples at war. Call her cynical but love seemed to her a fleeting emotion that couldn't withstand the vicissitudes of life.

Sylvie tossed off the bedcovers and winced at the sound of a pneumatic drill right outside her bedroom window. How long did it take to renovate a house, for pity's sake? This mind-scrambling, eardrum-bursting racket had been going on for nine months. What were the owners building? The Taj Mahal? Sylvie twitched the curtains aside to take a peek. The Victorian townhouse, which was adjacent and the twin of hers, was thankfully inching closer to completion but it seemed every tradesperson had turned up this morning for the final touches. She hadn't met the owners—no one seemed to know who was throwing a frightening amount of money at the Mayfair townhouse. Not like she could talk. Her house cost her a fortune three years ago, but owning her own home had been top of her to-do list since she was ten, and not a day went past when she wasn't thankful for her home and the one she had bought for her mother.

Sylvie turned from the window with a smile of satisfaction on her face. Even ear-splitting drills and jackhammers couldn't put a dent in her pride about rising above her poverty-stricken background to becoming one of London's most successful family lawyers with her own all-female practice. Who was it who said success was the best revenge? Sylvie didn't care who said it, but she hoped her pond scum father had heard it.

Half an hour later, Sylvie walked into the reception area of her law firm. Samira, one of the two secretaries, looked up from her computer and grimaced. 'Edwina Winters is here,' she said in an undertone, as the clients' waiting room was only a short distance away. 'She insisted on seeing you. Apparently, her husband has changed lawyers again.'

Sylvie frowned. 'Who's he got now?'

Samira gave her a look that sent a prickling shiver tiptoeing up the back of Sylvie's neck and over her scalp. 'Jack Wilde.'

Sylvie had perfected her poker face over the years of being a lawyer. Even long before her legal training, she had learned to disguise her emotions behind a mask of composure no young child should ever have to wear. But hearing Jack Wilde's name this early in the morning without a shot or two of caffeine on board was too much to handle without a tiny hairline crack in her poise.

'O-kay...' Sylvie let out an uneven breath, her pulse beginning to pound at the thought of another battle with Jack. She lost the last two court cases she'd had with him as her opponent. Could this be third time lucky for him? Was she in for another public humiliation?

Jack was a good lawyer who always fought hard for his clients. But then, so did she. Jack might be an attack dog lawyer, but she was a terrier with a bone and it took a hell of an opponent to get it off her. Trouble was, Jack Wilde was a hell of an opponent. Sylvie refused to think of him as her nemesis. She had faced down many arrogant male lawyers who thought they could wipe the floor with a young woman who only just scraped in at five foot five.

'I'll see Edwina in consulting room five,' Sylvie said. 'Can you call my first client and warn them I'll be a few minutes behind schedule?'

'Sure, will do.'

A short time later, Sylvie sat opposite a tearful Edwina Winters, who launched into a litany of her soon-to-be-ex-husband's bad behaviour. Listening to the list of narcissistic actions of Hugo Winters made Sylvie all the more determined to fight for Edwina and her two children to make sure they were not damaged by the war between their parents. Children were often the invisible victims in an acrimonious divorce and because Sylvie had lived experienced of it, she could pick up the signs at the get-go.

'So, the last mediation session,' Sylvie interjected

gently, trying to nudge her client out of the victim role and into a more proactive stance. 'How did it go? Were you able to come to any agreement on custody?'

Edwina blew her nose on a tissue and then tucked it up her sleeve. 'It was a disaster. Hugo painted me as a hopeless mother and then he stormed out and said he wouldn't be in another mediation session without his lawyer present. I found out last night he sacked his previous one and engaged the services of Jack Wilde.'

She started to cry again and hunted for her tissue and once she located it, wiped at her streaming eyes. 'E-everyone knows he's lethal in court. I'll lose custody of my babies. Hugo will tell Jack Wilde a whole pack of lies about me to paint me as an incompetent mother.'

'It might not get to court if we ask for another mediation session with both lawyers present,' Sylvie said, even though she was dreading any sort of session with Jack Wilde. But she figured it would be a lot less stressful facing him in a mediation meeting than in court like the last two times. The mediation sessions were private, court on the other hand was public. She could do without another public humiliation at Jack's hands.

Edwina wiped at her eyes with the back of her hand and Sylvie pushed a box of tissues on the desk closer to her. 'I'm trying to keep costs down but Hugo seems determined to take this all the way to court. How will I survive it? He's always handled the finances in our marriage. I have no idea how to find the funds to pay for months and months of legal advice. I've had to borrow heaps off my parents, but they can't really afford it and I'm not sure I'll be able to pay them back.'

'We have a payment scheme in place for people in your situation,' Sylvie said, thinking of her mother back in the day when there was no help at all. It was one of the things she was most proud of in her practice.

She wasn't running a charity by any means but she wouldn't allow her clients to be left destitute either. She and her colleagues kept costs down, especially for clients who were struggling, but Sylvie still was mindful she had a law firm to run with all the overheads of any other business. 'But try not to worry about that for the moment,' she went on. 'Let's aim for another mediation session and take things from there.'

Edwina dabbed at each of her eyes in turn and gave Sylvie a strained smile. 'Thank you for seeing me. I know you have back-to-back clients but I just couldn't get through another day of worry. I can't eat, I can't sleep and I didn't know what else to do.'

Sylvie rose from her chair, signalling the end of their session. 'I'm here for you anytime, Edwina. That's my job. I'll get my secretary to inform you of the date and time of the next mediation session. Take care of yourself.'

Once Edwina left the consulting room, Sylvie sat back down on a chair with a thump. She was already forty minutes late for her next client and she still hadn't had a shot of caffeine. Industrial-strength jackhammers were beginning to sound inside her head and she let out a strong curse word. 'You are *not* going to win this time, Jack Wilde,' she said to the four book-lined walls that surrounded her. 'No freaking way.'

A week later, Sylvie arrived early to the mediation counsellor's rooms but Edwina Winters had texted to say she would be late due to a hold-up with her teenage daughter's school drop-off. Jack Wilde sauntered into the waiting room two minutes after Sylvie sat down, but he too was on his own.

'Good morning, Ms Rathbone,' he said with a glinting smile that made her spine tighten with awareness.

His voice was rich and deep, with a gravel and honey thing going on and a generous dollop of Devonshire cream. The sort of voice she could listen to and fantasise about things she had no business fantasising about—especially with him. She had heard his Shakespearean court room voice and still been affected. He was mesmerising in every possible way a man could be. Damn him.

Part of the reason she avoided him was because she didn't trust herself around him. She found it hard not to stare at those incredible blue eyes. Found it near impossible not to gaze at his beautifully sculptured mouth that hinted at the potent sensuality of his nature. A notorious playboy who could have any woman he wanted was not Sylvie's idea of a date and yet…and yet…her pulse raced every time she saw him.

'Morning.' Sylvie tried not to notice the way his dark grey suit, crisp white shirt, and red-and-black-striped tie highlighted the unusual blue of his eyes. How was it even possible to have such attractive eyes?

A light ice blue with a dark outline around the iris, as if someone had meticulously defined it with a fine black felt-tip marker. His height and commanding presence made the waiting room shrink to the size of a shoebox. Standing, his head was dangerously close to the light fitting. Six foot four with broad shoulders and a trim figure, Jack Wilde was arrestingly, ravishingly, pulse-trippingly handsome. His jaw was square, his nose long and straight, and when he smiled two dimples appeared either side of his sensual mouth and laughter lines crinkled his eyes at the corners. His teeth were so white they showcased his tanned complexion like an advertisement for toothpaste and outdoor sports.

She had rarely seen him without a day or two of stubble, which gave him an arrantly masculine look that was heightened by his loosely styled wavy jet-black hair. So loosely styled, it looked like he had just combed it with his fingers. It gave him a rampantly rakish air that, compared to him, made the male models in sexy aftershave ads look like altar boys.

Speaking of aftershave, she could smell an alluring hint of his cologne, a woodsy and country leather combination that made her nostrils flare to take more of it in like a forbidden drug.

Sylvie forced her eyes away from his wide-spread, strongly muscled thighs but holding his gaze was even more challenging. Every time she tried, something hit her in the chest like a Taser beam. *Zzzttt.* There was a confident, some would say arrogant, gleam in his eyes that irked her considering their history. He knew he could win because he had already done so, while she was the underdog and had to summon as much confidence and determination as she could to go into battle with him again.

But her biggest battle was fighting her attraction to him. She wasn't the sort of woman to develop a crush. She had never been in love in her life and didn't intend to go down that path anytime soon. And yet… Jack Wilde made her feel things she had never felt before. Tingles of lust that stirred her blood into a feverish flood in her feminine flesh. How could a sensible no-nonsense professional woman such as herself be reduced to these primal urgings? Was it her long stint of celibacy? Had she left it too long between drinks, as the saying went? Her last so-called 'drink' had turned her off dating for months. Six to be exact.

'Where's your client?' Jack asked, taking the seat opposite her, his languid laid-back pose a stark contrast to her stiff upright posture.

'Running late with the school run. Where's yours?' Her tone was clipped and businesslike—no idle chit-chat for her. Jack Wilde was the enemy and she must not forget it, no matter what her wayward body thought.

Jack pushed back his sleeve to glance at his designer watch. 'Should be here any second.' He flashed her another heart-stopping smile. 'How's business?'

'Booming,' Sylvie said with a pert lift of her chin and a glacial stare. 'Yours?'

'Same.'

The door opened and Hugo Winters came in bringing with him an air of agitation that was palpable. He was a short man in his fifties who looked like he had

had one too many business lunches. Although he was wearing a designer suit, it did nothing to hide his considerable paunch, the buttons of his jacket straining against the fabric so much Sylvia was expecting one to pop off and ping across the room like a missile. His complexion was ruddy as if he was constantly in a state of emotional dysregulation. He had balding greying brown hair that he tried to disguise by sweeping a longer side portion across the bald spot that only drew more attention to it, like a coffee scroll had landed on his head.

The comparison between clock-stopping handsome, gym-toned Jack Wilde and his client was like a virile thoroughbred stallion with an overweight and bad-tempered Shetland pony. Sylvie wondered what her client had ever seen in Hugo Winters, but love was blind as they say. She, on the other hand, had twenty-twenty vision when it came to men. She was a card-carrying member of the most-men-are-bastards club. And she planned to stay that way.

'Edwina's late as usual,' Hugo muttered without bothering to greet either Jack or Sylvie.

'She'll be here in a minute or two,' Sylvie said, unintimidated by Hugo's boorish manner. 'Please take a seat. Nasreen will call us in soon.'

'Don't know why we have to go through this yet again. It's pointless because I'm never going to agree to Edwina's demands.' Hugo grumbled and plonked his bulk into one of the waiting-room chairs. Sylvie found herself holding her breath, hoping the antique chair could accommodate him without splintering into pieces.

She caught Jack's glinting gaze and felt a wave of heat course over her cheeks because she was seriously tempted to giggle. She *never* giggled. Not in front of clients or colleagues and certainly not in front of her enemy. She didn't want to share any sort of camaraderie with him. She wanted to keep her distance—a professional distance so she could get through this case without being sidetracked by Jack Wilde's alluring charm.

'Let's see if we can come to some agreement this time so you don't have to pay your lawyer hundreds and thousands of pounds,' Sylvie said, doing her best to avoid Jack's amused gaze, but it took a mammoth effort.

Just then a flustered Edwina came stumbling through the doorway, her face flushed, her chin-length bobbed blond hair looking like it had just been through a wind tunnel. She brushed it back from her face and clutching her tote bag like a shield against her body, said, 'Sorry, sorry, sorry. Mimi wasn't keen on going to school and it took me ages to talk her into going and then I had to stay with her to—'

'You're way too soft with her,' Hugo said with a contemptuous look that matched his tone. 'If you'd been firm with her in the first place, you wouldn't have to fuss over her like she's still three years old instead of thirteen.'

'Well, at least I don't shout and swear and threaten her,' Edwina shot back.

Sylvie mentally rolled her eyes. It was like déjà vu

listening to these two argue. Her parents had bickered non-stop pre- and post-divorce. She suspected if they still had contact with each other, they would continue to fight over which way the breeze was blowing.

Jack said nothing but she sensed him taking in the dynamic, assessing who had the balance of power in the relationship and how he would act in the best interests of his client. Sylvie had enough experience to know not all relationships were as they seemed on the surface. It took time to get to know your client and hear their story, but it was also important to save a part of your mind for the other party's version of events just to make sure you were not being manipulated or hoodwinked in any way.

Thankfully, the mediation counsellor Nasreen came out of her consulting room before World War Three began and invited them in with a brief formal smile. 'Good morning, please come in.'

Sylvie moved past Jack, who was waiting for her to precede him, and her arm accidentally brushed against his suit jacket. Even through layers of fabric, a lightning zap of energy passed from his body to hers, sending her senses into free fall. Even though she was wearing heels, he towered over her, and she knew she would end up with a crick in her neck if she looked up at him for too long. She stared ahead, schooled her features into her professional mask of confident competence, and entered the mediator's office with firm footsteps and a straight spine. *You've got this.* Saying it in her head was not as powerful as saying it aloud but she needed to believe she could beat Jack-damn-his-gorgeous-bedroom eyes-Wilde.

Jack breathed in the flowery scent of Sylvie Rathbone as soon as she entered the mediation room. Every time he saw her, he noticed something different about her. She had chestnut hair that she had pulled back in a tight bun which gave her an elegant ballerina vibe she probably hadn't intended.

She was always a little stiff and formal around him, which amused him immensely. She was a rare creature in that she didn't fawn over him as most women did and he liked it. He liked it a lot. It was refreshing to be in the company of someone who didn't see him as a potential lover. It ignited the thrill of the chase in him. A primal urge to see if he could win her over. He could feel the stirring of it deep in his groin—the pulse of lust that was triggered by her aloof and cool manner around him. But he had noticed the way her nutmeg-brown eyes drifted to his mouth and to his legs while they were sitting opposite each other. He felt the crackling tension in the air, an invisible current that zapped him as she brushed against him.

Jack jotted down notes as he listened to the mediation session. While he was all for saving money for his clients where possible, he loved the battle of the courtroom. The preparation, the challenge of fighting for his client, the theatre of court, the protocols and formality he worked to his advantage. Sometimes mediation worked and there was no need to take things any further, but he had a feeling his client Hugo Winters would not stop until he had taken Edwina to court.

It always intrigued him how two people who had vowed to love each other until death do us part ended up in court a few years later, tearing each other down until there was practically nothing left to divvy up. Had they been in love or lust? Was their love real or a fantasy?

Jack had never been in love so could not speak from experience but recently his younger brother Jago had reunited with his fiancée, Mollie, after she had jilted him two years prior. Jack was happy for Jago and approved of his choice of life partner, but he didn't want it for himself. He was having too much fun being a playboy with the freedom to do what he liked with whomever he liked.

Jack flicked his gaze to where Sylvie Rathbone was sitting, also taking notes, a small frown of concentration on her forehead. A strand of her hair had worked its way loose and she absently brushed it back, tucking it behind the dainty shell of her ear. She was wearing pearl stud earrings as creamy white as her skin. A pearl pendant on a fine gold chain hung from her gazelle-like neck, resting against the dove-grey silk of her blouse where her small but perfect breasts pushed against the fabric. She was wearing a pencil skirt and matching jacket, giving her a schoolmarm look that was potently attractive.

She had a touch-me-not air that drew him like a magnet to metal. He was so used to women giving him brazen come-on signals that it was amusing to be in the company of someone who appeared immune to him. But Jack wasn't one to rely solely on appearances.

Sylvie looked up from her notes as if she sensed his gaze on her. Her eyes widened a fraction and then her chin came up, her full mouth tightening and lightning flashing in her gaze. She arched her eyebrows in an imperious manner and a tingle ran down Jack's spine. He wasn't fooled by her ice-maiden façade. There was too much fire in her gaze for her to be frozen to the core. He would enjoy striking a spark with her and seeing how hot it would get between them.

'Are there any further questions?' the mediator began to draw the session to a close.

'Yes,' Sylvie said, clicking the ball-point pen in her hand three times. Click. Click. Click. Jack wasn't sure if it was a nervous thing or a way of getting everyone's attention. Whatever, it worked. He couldn't take his eyes off her, especially when she spoke. 'My client suspects her husband has assets hidden offshore that are not showing up in the settlement arrangement. I'd like to engage the services of an independent forensic accountant to make sure my client gets a fair share of the assets she has helped her husband to accrue over the fifteen years of their marriage.'

Jack rocked his own pen from side to side between his thumb and index finger, his gaze going to his client. Hugo Winters, who was giving a good impression of a man who had been falsely accused of a heinous crime. He opened and closed his mouth in shock, his hands gripping the arms of the chair he was sitting in, his expression darkening in outrage.

'I've given my solicitor every relevant document I possess,' Hugo said, glancing at Jack for verification.

Jack remained expressionless. He didn't particularly like Hugo Winters, but he was paid to act for him, to protect him from exploitation and to get the best deal for him. And he wasn't fooled by Edwina's 'poor me' victim role either. Call him cynical but he had a feeling there was more to this case than even Sylvie Rathbone suspected. Jack had only just been asked to act for Hugo Winters, so he hadn't had enough time to do a thorough rundown of everything Hugo and Edwina owned together or separately. Going into a battle underprepared was not Jack's way of doing things. He didn't win by being caught off guard. He didn't win by being taken for a fool. He won because he was good at reading people and getting all the facts on the table before he made up his mind.

'Do you have any objections to Ms Rathbone's suggestion?' the mediator asked Jack.

'Not at all,' Jack said, glancing at Sylvie with a confident smile.

She didn't return his smile but glared at him as if he had just crawled out of a primeval swamp with his knuckles dragging along the ground. A spark burned in Jack's groin, lighting a fire that spread throughout his body with hot flickering flames of lust. He set himself a challenge to melt the icy Sylvie Rathbone until she was molten lava in his arms.

CHAPTER TWO

SYLVIE WAS HOPING to slip away before she was cornered by her weeping client or her grinning and smug opponent, so she took the fire exit instead of the elevator. As she descended the stairs the click-clack of her heels echoed hollowly in the stairwell. Then she became aware of other footsteps following her—firm, determined, purposeful. She glanced around to see Jack Wilde on the level above her. He continued to close the distance between them, smiling down at her with his dimples showing and his eyes glinting.

Sylvie didn't want to appear intimidated by him by speeding up her pace, so she adopted a bored expression and waited for him on the landing above the next flight of stairs. 'You need me for something?'

The glint in his eyes sparkled like a fizzing firework, and something fluttered deep and low in her belly like a trapped moth. 'You could say that. Got time for a coffee?' he said with a smile that made her knees threaten to buckle.

'I have clients to see in half an hour.'

'One coffee. Deal?'

Sylvie would have refused but she was caffeine deprived and, besides, she wanted to know why Jack was not against a forensic accountant looking over Hugo Winters's financial affairs. He'd been surprisingly agreeable, which had come as a shock to her. Having anything to do with Jack would normally be a no-no for her. But in order to help her client, she needed to suss out her opponent in this complicated divorce settlement. What better way than meeting with Hugo Winters's solicitor so she could get a better handle on how Jack would approach things? But she didn't want to appear too eager. Jack had enough women saying yes to him without her joining the throng.

'Is it wise for our clients to see us having coffee together?' she asked. 'I wouldn't want Edwina to think I'm not solely committed to her best interests.'

Jack was now on the landing where she was and his height advantage was all the more apparent. She had to crane her neck to look up at him. But looking up at him was a mistake. A big mistake. His mouth was generous, hinting at his undoubtable sensual skill set. The bottom lip was a fraction fuller than the top and his white-toothed smile was highlighted by his dark stubble and the olive complexion of his skin.

She began to fantasise about how those lips would feel pressed hard against her own. How the stroke of his tongue would feel against hers, how his arms would feel wrapped around her, drawing her close to his superbly toned body. She hadn't been kissed in months. She had deleted the dating apps after her last disastrous date with an ego-tripping jerk who didn't stop talking about himself and his ex-partner the whole time. Being near Jack Wilde triggered something in her she didn't want triggered—desire. Raw, earthy, spine-tingling desire.

Jack was the last person she would consider becoming involved with, but then, that was a moot point because he didn't have relationships that lasted longer than a day or two. He was the king of the blink-and-you'd-miss-it fling and one-night stands. She considered it beneath her to join the long list of his lovers. She had pride on her side and she would cling to it with all her might.

Sylvie gave herself a mental slap for even thinking about Jack and his multitudinous lovers and raised her eyes to his. 'One coffee. I don't want to be late for my other clients.' She told herself she was tempted only by the prospect of caffeine and her interest in Jack's tactics, not his charming company.

'There's a café nearby. I know the owner. I'll get us a table away from the windows.'

Sylvie gave him a pointed look. 'Thank you. I would hate to have myself linked to you in any way other than professionally.'

Jack grinned as if she had complimented rather than insulted him. 'Come on. It's only a block from here.'

A short time later, Sylvie found herself sitting opposite Jack in a swish café that had a tempting array of pastries in a glass counter near the cash register, and the divine fragrance of freshly brewed coffee teasing her nostrils. Jack's friend Ben Blackwood turned out to be an old schoolmate and they greeted each other with one of those ridiculously complicated fist bump handshakes and wide smiles. Ben went to get their order, and while they were waiting for their coffee, Sylvie tried not to compare the two men, but Jack was by far the mostIt handsome and charming. He had a magnetic presence that made her spine tingle every time he looked at her.

She fought to disguise her reaction to him but wondered if he sensed it anyway. After all, he had a lot of experience when it came to women. Of the three Wilde brothers, Jack was the standout playboy. The press was often reporting on his latest fling, and he only had to be seen with someone once for speculation about his love life to go viral.

'How long were you at boarding school with your friend?' Sylvie asked to keep her mind from drifting into the dangerous territory of imagining what Jack was like as a lover.

'Eleven years.'

Sylvie raised her eyebrows. 'So, you went when you were…?' She didn't have time to do the maths before he answered.

'Seven, right after my parents were killed.' He spoke without emotion; it was as if he was simply reporting an event in the past that had little or no effect on him. But she could see a fleeting shadow pass through his blue gaze and there was no sign of his charming smile.

Their coffees arrived at that moment and Sylvie waited until the young waitress had left before probing a bit more. 'Were you all going to go to boarding school at some point even if your parents hadn't been killed?'

He gave a shrug of one broad shoulder and picked up his coffee cup, looking at the black liquid rather than meet her gaze. 'At some point, yes, but we went a little bit earlier than planned.' He lifted his coffee cup to his mouth, and she stared at his lips as they took a sip of the fragrant brew. She found herself thinking of his sensual lips touching hers, caressingly, drawing from her a response that no one else had been able to do.

She derided herself for her weakness. It was not like her to become obsessed with a man. She had never been in love, not even close. She had only felt the mildest stirrings of lust on dates with other men, and she had never been physically satisfied by sleeping with a date, which was one of the reasons she had stopped dating. Her period of celibacy was by choice and yet...*gulp*... Jack Wilde.

She watched him swallow another mouthful of coffee and then the tip of his tongue came out to brush across his lips and something hot and liquid pooled between her thighs. How could she get turned on by simply watching him drink coffee?

Sylvie picked up her own cup and took a sip and almost purred with relief as the caffeine hit her bloodstream. 'Whose idea was it to send you to boarding school? Your grandparents?'

Jack put his coffee cup back on his saucer with a clink of the china connecting. 'My grandfather's. My grandmother was against it, but his word was law.' He gave a crooked smile that didn't make the distance to his eyes and added, 'He likes to think it still is, but since his stroke a while back he's had to relinquish a bit more control than he likes.'

Sylvie took another sip of coffee, then put her cup down, absently stirring the liquid with a teaspoon even though she didn't take sugar. 'It must have been a terrible time for you and your younger brothers, not to mention your grandparents losing their only child.' She might not like Jack Wilde but she would be a monster not to feel some empathy for him being orphaned so young. It was amazing he had grown up confident and sure of himself after he had lost his parents so early in his life. Or had losing his parents made him step up, to grow up way before his time?

Another dismissive shrug of his broad shoulder. 'It was but I had to accept it and move on. I was lucky to have had my parents the longest given I'm the eldest son. Jago remembers them but Jonas, being only three at the time, has virtually no memories of them.'

He picked up his coffee cup again and met her gaze. 'What about your parents? Where do they live?' He kept his gaze trained on hers over the rim of his cup as he took another sip.

Sylvie put her teaspoon down on the saucer. 'My mother lives in Surrey. I don't have any contact with my father. Not since my parents divorced when I was ten.' *Why are you telling him anything about yourself?* It made her aware of how easily Jack could get under her guard. She would have to be careful around him. She didn't want him knowing every detail of her difficult childhood and the struggle it had been to overcome the poverty her father had thrown her and her mother into post-divorce.

Jack raised one dark eyebrow in an arc. 'Am I right in guessing that's what motivated you to become a divorce lawyer?'

Sylvie gave a tight smile. 'It's one of the reasons but not the only one.'

'What are some of the others?'

She gave him a frosty look. 'Aren't we here to discuss the Winterses' divorce instead of talking about our life stories?'

'You started the back-story discussion.' He said it without rancour and his smile had returned to its most charismatic.

Sylvie ignored his comment and veered the subject back to where she wanted it. 'Why did you accept my request for an independent forensic accountant? I thought you'd push back on that, especially as you've only just been engaged by Hugo Winters. You haven't had much time to look over everything.'

'I work well under pressure.'

'I'm sure you do but how well do you know your client? Or do you possess magical people-reading skills?'

Jack gave one of his short and way too attractive laughs. His gaze ran over her tightly set features, and she forced herself to sit in a more relaxed pose. She didn't want him to read her like a bestselling novel, but his intelligent gaze was unsettling, and she felt exposed in a way she had never felt with anyone else. It was like he could see through the armour she had wrapped herself in to keep her past private.

She hated thinking of that bewildered little ten-year-old girl who had adored her father but then been cast aside, along with her mother, as if she meant nothing to him. Something about Hugo Winters reminded her of her father and she was going to do everything in her power to stop what happened to her from happening to Edwina and her children.

'I've met men in his situation hundreds of times before,' Jack said. 'He wants full custody of his children because he doesn't believe his wife is capable of parenting them properly.'

Sylvie frowned. 'You've only met Edwina once. How can you possibly make such a judgement on a single meeting?'

'It sounds like she has weak boundaries when it comes to the kids,' Jack said. 'The school refusal for instance.'

Sylvie made a scoffing sound. 'What? You think she should just push the kid out of the car on the way past the school? What do you know about teenage girls? It's a tricky time of life and the tough love approach doesn't work. What if something else is going on for Mimi? Bullying for instance? Mental health issues? There are heaps of reasons she might be refusing to go to school.'

'What if it's just good old-fashioned attention-seeking?' Jack said. 'When a kid's parents are in the process of divorcing it can be hard on everyone, but the girl's acting up isn't going to make her parents fall in love with each other again. Hugo is done. He wants out. And he wants the kids in order to protect them.'

Sylvie screwed up her lips in disgust. 'He only wants the kids to punish Edwina. Surely you can see that?'

Jack's expression gave nothing away. 'He wants the kids so that they aren't poisoned against him by their mother.'

Sylvie pushed her coffee cup away as if it tasted vile. 'You're so damn biased. You've only heard his version of the story. He's painting Edwina in an appalling light so he can win. He doesn't care about the kids. He done practically nothing towards their upbringing apart from providing for them. Men like him make me sick to my stomach.'

Jack rocked back in his chair, a cynical smile tilting one side of his mouth. 'Now who's sounding biased?'

She glared at him hotly enough to froth his coffee, except he had it black. 'The reason I run an all-female law practice is to represent women who otherwise wouldn't have a chance of fair and just representation. The legal system claims to be fair but we both know justice isn't what happens in court—it's who spins the most convincing narrative.'

'Hugo Winters is my client and it's my job to get him the best deal I can. I don't have to like the guy. I just have to win his case.'

Sylvie gave him a scathing look. 'Winning at any cost?'

Jack gave her one of his annoyingly confident smiles. 'Yep.'

She ground her back teeth until her jaw ached. 'Well, Jack Wilde, I'd like to remind you that young and vulnerable children are involved in this divorce case. They are not just chess pieces you can move around a board. They are kids whose parents' divorce will have a lifelong impact on them if it's not conducted in a fair and just manner. This isn't a game of win or lose, it's a fight to protect a mother and her children from a coercive and controlling bully who seems to have pulled the wool of a whole flock of flipping sheep over your eyes.'

Sylvie pushed back her chair and opening her purse, threw some money on the table. 'Thank you for the chat,' she said through tight lips. Then she turned on her heels and stalked out before he could have the last word.

Jack glanced at the note she had tossed on the table, then back at Sylvie as she wove around the café tables for the exit. He couldn't take his eyes off her small, elegant figure with her head held in a haughty manner. What she lacked in height, she made up for in spades with attitude and feistiness. He admired her spirit, her determination and drive, which were so like his own approach to life, but the thrill of winning for his clients had to come before anything else. He couldn't allow himself to be distracted by her on a personal level. But the thought of a fling with her was so exciting he could feel the tingle of anticipation deep in his groin. Mixing business and pleasure wasn't his normal modus operandi. He liked to keep his work life separate from his day job. No exceptions. But hot damn, this time he was tempted.

The Winterses' divorce could well be a long drawn-out one, which would mean Jack would have more contact with Sylvie over the following weeks if not months. He had won a couple of court cases against her, which he assumed was why she was so testy with him, but work was work. He didn't allow feelings to get in the way of a court battle. In fact, he didn't allow feelings to get in the way of anything.

Losing his parents so young had taught him to bury his emotions, to keep them contained so they couldn't bubble up to the surface and haunt him in ways he didn't want to be haunted. He was the eldest of the Wilde brothers, and even at the age of seven he had grasped what the tragedy of losing his parents meant for both him and his younger siblings. He was going to have to be tough, invincible, resilient. He would have to be strong for his brothers. He grieved but in his own private way. His grandfather had not allowed him and his brothers to rely on each other and had sent them to different boarding schools to toughen them up. Jack had coped with it, but he wasn't sure it had been the best approach for Jago and Jonas.

More recently, Jago had gone through two years of hell after his fiancée jilted him, although they were now back together and planning a summer wedding once Jonas came home from his latest project. Jonas had cut all contact with the family for the last few months, supposedly working on some top-secret naval architect contract, but Jack's natural tendency for scepticism made him wonder if something else was going on. But it wasn't the first time Jonas had gone to ground, and it likely wouldn't be the last. Jonas was a solitary person who had taught himself not to need others.

Jack's mate Ben came over to the table carrying a tray of used cups and reached down to pick up Sylvie's empty one. 'Did your lady friend give you the brush-off? You must be losing your touch, mate.'

Jack gave a crooked smile. 'We're colleagues, not lovers.'

Ben's smile was teasing. 'How soon before that changes, eh?'

The tingling in Jack's groin stirred again at the thought of mixing business with pleasure with feisty little Sylvie Rathbone. 'I get the feeling she hates my guts. I won a couple of cases against her. Not sure she's going to forgive me for that.' He kept his tone light and playful.

Ben laughed. 'What woman you've wanted has ever said no to you? I bet it won't be long before you score with her.'

For some reason his mate's words didn't sit comfortably with Jack. It made him sound like a trophy hunter, looking to carve out another notch on his bedpost. Yes, he was a playboy who changed lovers faster than most people, but he didn't see Sylvie as a casual once-only hook-up, although he wasn't sure why. She wasn't someone who would disappear from his life like someone from a dating app. They moved in the same circles, they encountered each other at the law society functions, including the Summer Fundraiser Masked Ball this coming Saturday, which was being held at his brother Jago's fancy hotel right here in London.

Jack picked up his coffee cup and drained it, then handed it to Ben across the table. 'The case we're working on looks like it could drag on for months. Anyway, I don't know if she already has a partner.'

'That hasn't stopped you in the past.' Ben said it playfully, but it still made Jack mentally cringe. To his shame he had slept with a married woman once, but only because she had lied and told him her marriage was over. However, he still felt he had failed himself by indulging in a one-night stand with her. He had crossed a moral line he had not wanted to cross. He liked casual dating for the simple transaction of pleasure between two consenting adults. But to engage in an affair with someone who was with someone else was something he always avoided.

Jack pushed back his chair and stood. 'How are Yasmin and the twins?' Nothing like a quick change of subject to get away from his troubling thoughts.

'They're great, although they're both teething at the moment.' Ben grimaced and added, 'I can't remember the last time I had a full night's sleep but it's worth it. The twins are starting to talk, and Ellie took her first steps on the weekend. Ethan is still cruising the furniture, but it won't be long before he lets go. You should come over sometime, have dinner with us. It's a bit of a circus and food goes everywhere but it's fun.'

Jack smiled back. 'I'll wear a hazmat suit, then, shall I?'

Ben chuckled. 'You do that.'

CHAPTER THREE

SYLVIE WORKED HER way through her list of clients until lunchtime. Thankfully a couple of clients only needed half an hour of her time, so she was able to make up the time she had lost whilst having coffee with Jack Wilde. It still shocked her that she had gone with him but somehow, he made her forget about her boundaries where men were concerned. She was drawn to him against her will, against her reason and common sense. It was like he was a mystery she wanted to solve and while avoiding him wasn't going to solve anything, spending time with him was enticing danger into her life, the sort of danger she could do without.

On the surface Jack was confident and cocky, yet she couldn't help feeling there was more to him than that charming, easy-going lad about town. A depth to his character he let few people see. He was self-reliant, resilient and resourceful as a result of losing his parents so young. And that spoke to her, reminding her of her own loss, her own wounded inner child who had struggled to understand why her father had stopped loving her as easily as if he had flicked a switch.

Jack spoke of the loss of his parents without emotion, but she sensed the emotions were there all the same, pushed down deep inside him where they could no longer hurt him. She recognised it because it was what she did—smothered her emotions until they were silenced. But every now and again there was a whisper in her bones, reminding her of their presence and the damage they could do if she were to let them bubble to the surface.

Sylvie joined two of her colleagues, Natasha and Mariah, in the staff room kitchen, where they were seated chatting about a settlement they had just completed. They both looked up and smiled as she came in.

'So, how goes the War of the Winters?' Mariah asked.

Sylvie rolled her eyes and turned to take a coffee cup from the cupboard above the sink. Although she was not the sort of person who easily blushed, she could feel warmth heating her cheeks. Should she tell her workmates about her meeting with Jack?

'I have a feeling it's going to be one of those long, drawn-out affairs.' She poured herself a coffee and brought it over to the table and sat opposite Natasha and Mariah, cradling the cup in both of her hands. 'Hugo Winters doesn't seem to care how much money he spends on his hotshot lawyer as long as he gets custody of the kids. God, I hate men who use their kids as a means to an end. He doesn't care about them, he only cares about winning and so does his lawyer.'

Natasha reached for a rice cracker on the plate in front of her and nibbled on it for a moment. 'How old are the kids?'

'Thirteen and eleven—a girl and a boy. It's the teenage girl I'm most concerned about,' Sylvie said. 'Edwina Winters was late to the mediation meeting because Mimi was refusing to go to school. Apparently, it's not the first time either.'

Mariah let out a sigh. 'Sometimes I wonder why I chose this career. It's the kids that really get to me. They're collateral damage in most cases.'

'Me too,' Natasha said with feeling. 'But our legal firm's goal is to make divorce as seamless and painless as possible and to help women rebuild their lives.' She rubbed a hand over her swollen abdomen and shifted in her chair.

'Are you okay, love?' Mariah asked in concern.

Natasha took her wife's hand and gave it a reassuring squeeze. 'It's just Braxton Hicks contractions. It's pretty normal at this stage of the pregnancy.'

Sylvie couldn't help feeling a tiny pang of envy at the love her colleagues shared. They had been married two years and were expecting their first child in a month's time. While Sylvie had not envisaged marriage and children as part of her future, it didn't stop her feeling a twinge of regret her childhood had made her so adamantly against settling down with someone. What were the guarantees love would work out in the end? Nearly fifty percent of all marriages ended in divorce. How could she be sure she wouldn't end up part of those depressing statistics? No one gave you lessons on how to have a good marriage. You just dived right in as most of her clients had, believing love would conquer all. But life was not like in the fairy tales where everything turned out in the end. The Winterses were an example of what could happen when one person lost interest in the other. How could you ever trust the person you loved would continue to love you for as long as you both lived? Her father had loved her and her mother until he did not. The shock of it still stung Sylvie even after all these years. And her mother had never recovered from that shock. She had never dated another man, instead living a life of loneliness, still grieving the loss of her marriage and still feeling a failure, like it was somehow her fault. It seemed to Sylvie love was a switch in some people. They could turn it on and off at will, while others lived the rest of their lives wounded by the withdrawal of love. Her solution was to not love anyone so much as to be devastated by their disappearance from her life. The one and only exception she made was her love of her mother. Her mother had made huge sacrifices for her and Sylvie knew how fortunate she was to have at least one reliable and stable parent.

Her mind drifted back to Jack Wilde and his brothers who had lost both of their parents in a plane crash on a weekend away together. Sylvie was not a psychologist, but she suspected Jack's cynical approach to life and his playboy lifestyle were the hoof-prints of unresolved grief. But what was she doing thinking about Jack Wilde? He was her legal opponent in an acrimonious divorce, so it was imperative to keep her distance, to maintain a professional attitude at all times.

'Have you got your mask sorted for the fundraiser ball on Saturday?' Natasha asked. 'We're going to give it a miss because of the pregnancy. I can barely make it through the day, let alone dining and dancing the night away.'

'I have a Venetian mask I bought in Venice with my mother a couple of years ago,' Sylvie answered.

Mariah got a suggestive twinkle in her eyes. 'Are you taking a partner to the ball?'

Sylvie screwed up her face. 'No way. I deleted all my dating apps months ago. I've made a vow of celibacy for six months.'

'Do you know if Jack Wilde is going?' Natasha asked, with a similar sparkle in her eyes as Mariah's.

Sylvie schooled her features into an impassive expression even though the very mention of Jack's name was enough to get her senses flustered. 'I have no idea, nor do I care.'

Natasha and Mariah exchanged a look.

'What?' Sylvie asked, scowling at them both. 'He's probably going to bring some glamorous supermodel type as usual.' She rose from her chair and took her coffee cup to the sink and rinsed it and left it to drain on the dish rack.

'He's also highly likely to make a generous donation, not that he would broadcast it like other people would do,' Mariah said. 'He made a huge anonymous donation last year. The biggest of any other donor.'

Sylvie couldn't stop her eyebrows from lifting in surprise. 'Really? How did you find out if he made it anonymously?'

'I have my connections,' Mariah said with a mercurial smile.

Sylvie frowned. 'He might be generous but he's still arrogant and annoying.' She picked up her bag and slung the strap over one shoulder, giving her colleagues a quick smile. 'See you in the morning.'

'Have a good night. Are you doing anything special?' Natasha asked.

'It's my hot yoga night,' Sylvie said, already looking forward to the chance to stretch out her tight muscles. And to do something that took her mind off work… and Jack Wilde.

'Well, at least you'll get all hot and sweaty even if it's not with a guy,' Mariah said with a laugh.

Sylvie couldn't remember the last time she had been with anyone who had the potential to make her feel hot and sweaty…other than Jack Wilde, but she was not going to think about him.

Jack stayed back at his office so he could triple-check everything Hugo Winters had given him on his financial affairs. The Winterses certainly lived a lavish lifestyle but who was he to talk? Jack was born into wealth and was aware of the privileges he had, despite the tragic loss of his parents.

He would never admit this to anyone, most especially his brothers, but he sometimes wondered if the loss of his parents had helped him rather than disadvantaged him. He'd had to grow up and fast, learn how to navigate the world to best protect himself and his brothers from their overly critical grandfather. It had given him a strength of will, the drive and motivation to succeed no matter what obstacles were in his way.

Out of the three brothers, his win-at-all-costs personality was perhaps a little more like his grandfather's, but unlike his grandfather, Jack knew where to draw the line. Would he have had that same drive if he had grown up with his two loving parents? It was so hard to say.

His parents had been loving and generous with gifts and exotic holidays and yet he had always been conscious of their devotion to each other being more of a priority than their three sons. Jack's grandfather Maxwell referred to Jack's father's love for his mother as an obsession, and he still blamed that obsession for their deaths.

Maxwell had even had the temerity to accuse Jack's brother Jago of being obsessed with Mollie, his fiancée, when anyone could see they were well-suited and were better together than apart. Jack had never seen Jago so happy and content before, although he and Mollie were getting a little frustrated their much-longed-for wedding was on hold until Jonas came back from wherever he was currently working. Jack was not by nature a worrier but even his laid-back approach to life was being challenged by his youngest brother's lack of contact over the last few months.

Jack continued to work through the paperwork Hugo Winters had given him, making notes as he went. After another hour, he scraped his hair off his forehead and leaned back in his chair with a sigh. He was starting to realise the Winterses' divorce was going to be a lot more complicated than he had expected. It could take months to sort out the division of assets that were on paper, let alone the ones Sylvie suspected Hugo had secreted away out of sight via clever accounting.

He logged off his computer and pushed back his chair and stood, glancing outside his office window overlooking the view of the city. A light shower of rain had fallen an hour ago but now the sun was back from behind the clouds, casting a golden glow over the park near his office building. Summer had started in its tentative way, the evenings lengthening so families could make the most of the extra daylight. Jack decided to make the most of it too.

Sylvie got home after her hot yoga session and breathed a sigh of relief the workmen next door had finished for the day. She went out to her back garden, which was her pride and joy. Having lived on a council estate as a child, with only concrete to play on, it was a statement of her success she now had her own green space and so did her mother in Surrey. The garden was a combination of cottage flowers and hedged borders and a small vegetable patch and herb garden. Sylvie watered a couple of the pots while waiting for her little visitor to appear from over the fence.

The same time each day, a young stray cat she had called Shadow would cautiously enter her garden and wait in the shadows of a weeping birch tree for Sylvie to put down some food for her. Sylvie surmised the cat was female because of her grey-based tortoiseshell coat. The cat had a white bib and white paws and was only half grown. Sylvie suspected the cat was abandoned rather than feral for she seemed to want to connect with Sylvie with a look of yearning in her big green eyes. But Sylvie couldn't get close enough to the cat to touch her, because as soon as she approached, the cat would give a warning hiss and then disappear, hiding behind a shrub or hedge until Sylvie backed away. Then, driven by hunger, the little cat would cautiously approach the food, eat ravenously, and between mouthfuls check that Sylvie wasn't coming any closer.

Sylvie was patient and enjoyed the challenge of hopefully, over time, winning the little cat's trust. All the activity and noise next door was interrupting her taming process but at least she could spend the long early summer evenings sitting out with a glass of wine, far enough away to allow the cat the comfort of food without threatening her by trying to get too close too soon.

Sylvie left her glass of wine on the sandstone flagstones near her pots of scarlet-coloured geraniums and purple stocks, and walked over to the fence that divided her property from the neighbouring one. She stretched up on tiptoe and, clinging with her fingertips to keep her balance on the fence, she peered over, pleased to see the extension to the back of the Victorian townhouse was more or less complete. The kitchen/living room had an open-plan theme with lots of glass overlooking the garden, which at this point only consisted of a Japanese maple tree.

The rest of the garden would need some work, which would no doubt involve more noise and disruption, but at least that would mostly happen during work hours, so Sylvie wouldn't have to listen to it. She was about to let go of the fence when she caught sight of a tall man entering the new kitchen/living room area and her heart slammed against her breastbone like a wildly tossed hammer.

'Oh no!' Sylvie hadn't even realised she had gasped the words out loud, nor did she realise the person inside the new extension had such superb hearing, but he turned his head and saw her staring at him and smiled, and opened the bifold doors to come outside.

Sylvie let go of the fence and landed with a thump of her feet to the ground that reverberated through her body like a shock wave. Or maybe the shock wave was more to do with the fact that Jack Wilde was her new neighbour. Of all the houses in London, why had he bought the one next to hers? Had he been aware of who lived next door? She didn't know whether to be furious or relieved she had at least got someone living beside her she knew, rather than a complete stranger but still… *Jack Wilde?*

Sylvie was wearing her workout gear and hadn't showered since her hot yoga session. Her hair was a sweaty mess piled up on top of her head. Her cheeks were probably still red from pushing her body to the limit. She had only ever seen Jack whilst wearing work gear, her professional uniform of tailored clothing, her face lightly made-up, lipstick on, not a hair out of place. But here and now, every line and contour of her body could be seen in her yoga gear. She might as well be naked.

'Hey, nice evening,' Jack said, sauntering over to the fence that divided the two properties. Of course, he didn't have to stand on tiptoe and cling to the fence with his fingernails. His head and shoulders and half his muscled chest cleared it easily. 'So, you're my neighbour, huh?'

Sylvie hoisted her chin and glared at him. 'Are you telling me you didn't already know that?'

His smile made his eyes twinkle and laughter lines appear at the corners, as well as those attractive dimples. 'I did my research before I bought the property. Due diligence and all that.'

Sylvie ground her teeth. How long had he known? Months and months? She had done a council search as soon as the house was sold but had only come up with a trust name and it certainly wasn't the name Wilde. 'Why didn't you say something, like when we had coffee?'

'I thought I'd surprise you.'

'I hate surprises.'

He gave a mock-apologetic smile. 'I hope you're not too disappointed. If it's any reassurance, I'm not home much. Most days, I only come home to fall into bed.'

'Oh? With a new woman every night?' Her tone was reproachful, like a moralising Sunday school teacher from the eighteenth century.

His smile widened and the twinkle in his eyes became a devilish glint. 'I promise to keep the noise down.'

Sylvie could feel a blush staining her cheeks and was mortified he was witnessing it. 'Likewise,' she said, throwing him a look that suggested she was a female version of him, when in fact, she had never brought someone home. She didn't like any casual dates finding out where she lived.

Jack swept his gaze over her garden with its overflowing pots and neat hedges and flowers and herbs. 'It looks like you've got green thumbs, or do you get someone to do it for you?'

'I enjoy gardening. I'm self-taught but I get by.'

'Impressive.'

A long silence descended between them, broken only by the sound of the birds twittering in the shrubbery, preparing for nesting for the evening, and the drone of traffic on the streets out front.

She saw Jack glance towards her half-drunk glass of wine next to her geranium pot. 'I don't suppose you have a spare wine glass?'

She arched her brow in an imperious manner. 'I guess that's a change from asking for a cup of sugar.'

'Never touch the stuff. I'm sweet enough.' His grin was kryptonite weakening her willpower to keep her distance.

'Would you like a glass of wine?' The invitation was out before she could get her brain to list the reasons why socialising with him was not such a great idea.

'How neighbourly of you.' He launched himself over the fence with an agility that would have made a world champion gymnast envious. He was wearing a close-fitting white T-shirt that highlighted his muscular chest and forearms, and his dark blue jeans clung to his lean hips and strong thighs in a way that made her acutely aware of his maleness.

Sylvie drew in a tight little breath and backed away,

waving to the garden seat close to the back door. 'Erm, would you mind waiting here while I… I freshen up?' She pulled her sticky top away from her stomach but then wished she hadn't because his gaze followed the movement of her hand. 'I've been to a workout class and haven't had time to—'

'Take your time.' He sat on the wooden bench, crossed one ankle over his other leg and leaned back as if he was completely at home. Damn his confidence. Damn his arrogant assurance she would invite him in against her will, against her better judgement, against the warning bells of her conscience that saw him as a threat to her equilibrium.

'I'll get you a glass of wine first, of course.' Sylvie walked inside and poured a generous slug of the Pinot Grigio into a wine glass, then went back out and handed it to him. He took it from her but in doing so, his fingers brushed against hers, sending a shower of sparks from her fingers to her feminine core like a lightning strike. His ice-blue eyes met hers for a nanosecond, something in them warning her she had stepped into dangerous territory. There was a throb of tension in the air that was palpable.

She had crossed a boundary she hadn't intended to cross with Jack Wilde. What was she thinking inviting him to wait for her to have a shower? What was the point? She didn't want to be friends with him or neighbourly…although that seemed a bit petty. It was strangely comforting to know who was going to be living right next door to her, even if it was someone she didn't particularly like.

Sylvie went back inside her house and headed for her en suite upstairs. She groaned when she caught a glimpse of herself in the mirror above the basin. Her sweat-soaked hair was plastered to her head; any make-up she had applied earlier in the day had smudged beneath her eyes or completely disappeared, and her cheeks had two red circles that might have been a post-workout flush, but she suspected had more to do with her handsome visitor waiting for her downstairs. Argh.

CHAPTER FOUR

JACK SIPPED HIS wine and listened to the evening sounds of Sylvie's thriving garden. He had never taken her for a green-thumb type as her hands were always neatly manicured and her nails painted a soft pink. But he knew how stressful being a lawyer was, especially one who dealt mostly with divorce. Like doctors, lawyers were not encouraged to allow their emotions to cloud their judgement. It was a tough gig—at times you had to make challenging decisions that not everyone was happy about, but the law was the law. Having some sort of hobby or recreational outlet was a wise choice in such a demanding career.

As much as Jack tried not to think about it, he could not stop his mind from imagining Sylvie upstairs showering away her workout perspiration. He had never seen her so casually attired before. Without her formal tailored clothes and neat hair and make-up, he had seen a different side to her that sparked his interest even further. Her close-fitting workout gear clung to her slight curves in all the right places, leaving nothing to his imagination. When she handed him the wine, he had caught a faint whiff of her heated body, the scent flaring his nostrils and sending a wave of warmth through his blood that was still thrumming in his veins.

Jack took another sip of wine and breathed in the scent of night-scented stocks to the right of where he was sitting. There was another pot full of scarlet geraniums a few feet away. He wasn't much of a gardener having been brought up on his grandparents' expansive estate tended by a team of gardeners, but even he could not ignore the intoxicating scent with its delicate hint of cloves. The garden was a mix of formality and casualness, structure and looseness that hinted at the complexity of its owner's personality.

Jack glanced towards the back of the garden and something small and furtive darted out of sight behind a shrub. He narrowed his gaze, wondering if he should warn Sylvie of the rat he thought he had seen earlier in his own back garden. Worksites were notorious for attracting vermin, especially when some of the workmen doing his house had not been as tidy about their food scraps as he would have liked.

When Jack heard Sylvie approach, he stood and turned to look at her. She had pulled her still damp hair back from her face in a high ponytail and was now wearing slim-fitting blue jeans and an open white linen shirt with a black tank top underneath. She had not put make-up on other than a bit of lip gloss, which gave her a girl-next-door vibe that was completely different from her more formal work look. Her feet were in slip-on sandals with heels that lengthened her slim legs and showcased her neatly painted toenails in a pink a shade or two darker than her fingernails. He could smell the fruity smell of her shampoo and conditioner, and he wondered if he would ever look at an apple or strawberry again without thinking of her.

Whoa, buddy. Put the brakes on. You're just interested in a fling, remember? His rational mind gave him a stern reminder but still he couldn't take his eyes off her. She was even more beautiful with wet hair and without the make-up and expertly tailored clothes.

Sylvie glanced at his barely touched glass of wine before meeting his gaze. 'Would you like a top-up?'

'No, this is fine. I was waiting for you to join me.'

There was a look of something in her eyes that told him she had noted the good manners his grandparents had drummed into him. 'Thank you.' She sat on the wooden seat as far away from him as possible and Jack smiled to himself. The challenge of winning her over was not going to be easy to achieve but it would be even more satisfying once he did. He didn't doubt that he would accomplish his goal. It wasn't in his nature to give up at the first hurdle. The thrill of the chase was zinging through his body like an electric current. He was turned on by her cool manner towards him because he sensed it was a defence mechanism, a wall she had built around herself.

Jack waited for her to pick up her wine glass before he picked up his. He watched her lips as they pursed on the rim of the glass to take a sip, then the up and down movement of her elegant, swan-like neck as she swallowed. The evening light cast a glow over her heart-shaped face and her eyes appeared as dark as chocolate.

Jack tilted his own glass to sip his wine, then held

it in his hand, nodding towards the back of the garden. 'I hope you're not squeamish about these things, but I thought I saw a rat a moment ago.'

Sylvie's eyes rounded in horror, and she gave a little shudder, which made the wine in her glass splash against the sides like a tidal wave in a teacup. 'A…' she gulped '…rat? Where?'

He pointed to the back of the garden. 'Down there. I didn't get a good look because it darted out of sight, but I saw one in my garden when I called in briefly last night.'

'Are you sure it was a rat? The one in your garden, I mean?'

'I know a rat when I see one.' Jack couldn't stop a shudder of his own. He wasn't a big fan of the creatures, but he would man up and do the right thing if Sylvie needed one disposed of…even if his gut roiled at the thought.

Her eyes surveyed the back garden for a long moment before she brought her gaze back to his. 'Are you sure it wasn't a cat? A small greyish tortoiseshell one?'

'Do you have one?'

Sylvie twisted her mouth in a wry manner. 'Well, not really, but I've been trying to tame a stray one. She's only young and is starving.'

'How do you know it's female?'

'The colour. Tortoiseshells are generally female, and gingers are generally male. It's a genetic thing.'

'How close have you got to her?'

'Not close enough to pat her. She runs away as soon

as I approach, but she always comes back, once I keep my distance, to get the food.'

'How long have you been feeding her?'

'Six weeks.'

Jack whistled through his teeth, marvelling at her patience. He would have called the RSPCA weeks ago. 'What if she has kittens before you catch her? A one-cat problem will become a five- or six-cats problem. Female cats can get pregnant in their first season.'

Sylvie's expression soured as if she had just been forced to listen to a biology lecture she hadn't wanted to hear. 'I know all that. I just wanted to see if I could catch her before that happens. And I would have if it hadn't been for all the noise from your place next door. It's been unbearable. I've been woken up each morning for months to the sound of jackhammers and drills, not to mention the tradesmen's radio blasting at full volume.'

'Renovations take time and a lot of money to do well,' Jack said. 'But there are strict guidelines about the hours each day power tools can be used. If any of my workmen have contravened those rules, please send me dates and times and recordings of their activity.' He gave her house a cursory glance and added, 'You do have a security system, don't you?'

Sylvie rolled her eyes and stood from the garden bench; her wine glass clutched in one hand. 'Of course I do. Now, I mustn't keep you.' She gave the fence a pointed glance and added. 'You must have lots to do to settle in.'

'A bit but it will only be a day or two before I'm

sleeping next door.' He tossed back the contents of his glass and then handed it to her. 'Thanks for the drink.' His smile was crooked but no less charming. 'Would you like a look around sometime?'

Sylvie gave him a stiff smile. 'I wouldn't want to intrude on your privacy.'

Jack could tell she was tempted but was trying to keep her distance. 'I'll invite you over when I've got it all set up.'

She chewed at her lower lip for a moment, a shadow of worry in her eyes. 'Do you really think it was a rat you saw?' There was a thread of uneasiness in her voice.

Jack could feel his skin crawling at the thought of having to deal with a rodent the size of a cat. He'd read somewhere that London apparently had more rats than people. Scary thought. He fought back a shudder of disgust. 'Don't worry. Maybe it was your little cat. Have you given her a name?'

'Shadow.'

He gave an approving nod. 'I'll keep an eye out for her.'

'Thank you.'

There was a moment of silence.

Jack found his gaze lowering to her mouth and wondering what it would feel like to kiss her soft lips. She had generous lips set in an oval face, with prominent dark brows that framed her beautiful nutmeg-brown eyes. Her eyelashes were naturally long and dark and her nose a gentle ski slope. Her slightly wavy chestnut hair was luxuriously abundant, and he longed to run his fingers through it to see if it felt as silky as it looked.

'Can I ask you something?' Sylvie's voice jolted him out of his intense study of her features.

'Sure. Fire away.'

She moistened her lips and his groin tightened. 'Why isn't your name on the property deed?'

Jack raised his brows. 'So, you *did* do your research.'

'I wanted to know who my neighbour was, yes, but all I came up with was a trust name. Fairlight or something like that. I can't quite remember.'

'Fairbright,' Jack said. 'It was my mother's maiden name. Both my parents came from wealthy families, and a trust fund was set up in the event of her death.'

'Are your maternal grandparents still alive?'

'Unfortunately, no. And we didn't see them much growing up because my maternal grandfather blamed my father for my mother's death, which of course annoyed my paternal grandfather.' Jack twisted his mouth in a rueful manner. 'Complicated, huh?'

'Yes, well, families often are.'

'Yep.'

Another silence.

Jack's eyes met Sylvie's in the growing darkness. A soft breeze disturbed the silence, the rustling leaves of the shrubbery whispering their nighttime secrets.

'I'd better let you get on with your evening,' Jack said. 'Thanks again for the drink.'

Sylvie didn't respond other than with a stiff sort of smile. But he wasn't daunted by her standoffish manner. He could be patient when he needed to be. He had decided he wanted her, and he sensed her interest in him despite her cool treatment of him so far.

Once Jack had vaulted back over the fence to his own property, Sylvie let out a breath she hadn't realised she was holding. Jack was her neighbour. She not only had to work with him, but she also now had to live next to him. She had a ringside seat to all his comings and goings and would be witness to all the stunning women he brought home.

Sylvie sighed and looked towards the back wall of her garden, a fine shiver lifting her skin in tiny goose bumps. She was sure Shadow was a cat, of course she was…but what if there were rats around? She gave an involuntary shudder and turned and went back inside her house, closing and locking the door with extra care. Cats she could handle, even wild ones, but rats?

No. No. No.

CHAPTER FIVE

The night of the summer fundraiser ball arrived but Sylvie was in two minds whether to go or not. Given that she had already made a hair appointment and had bought a stunning dress weeks ago, she talked herself into attending for the sake of raising funds for a worthy cause. She decided she would make an appearance, buy something ridiculously expensive from the silent auction and hope she could keep her mask on the whole night.

Sylvie arrived at the luxurious hotel owned by Jack's brother Jago and couldn't help admiring the décor. It was a grand style with lots of brass and marble and ankle-deep carpets in the bar area, but the ballroom was something on another level entirely, especially decked out for the Summer Fundraiser Ball. The room was festooned with silver and white helium balloons arranged in weighted trees both on the tables and at various places around the room. It gave the room a bridal atmosphere, especially with the whimsical flower arrangements adorning each corner of the room at various heights. One was taller than Sylvie even though she was wearing her highest heels. Garlands of silver and white satin ribbons adorned every chair and crystal chandeliers glittered and tinkled above the tables like delicate bunches of pendulous diamonds.

Most of the guests had already arrived and were either sipping champagne in the area outside the ballroom or making their way to the tables. Sylvie hoped she would be sitting by someone who would do all the talking, because she didn't feel like making conversation. She wasn't much of a social butterfly, and if anyone asked her to dance, she had already decided she would pretend she had sprained her ankle.

Everyone was wearing a mask, some more elaborate than others. There were stage masks, Hollywood film characters, cartoon and superheroes and fairy tale characters, and a collection of Venetian masks, although none the same as Sylvie's as she had bought a traditional mask that had cost a fortune, but she loved its dramatic look. It was black and gold with a large black feather standing up high, surrounded by smaller ones that formed the headpiece from where a gold embossed veil fell with a drape of intricately woven black lace that entirely covered her face. Her eyes were shielded by both the lace and the gold painted mask that perched on her nose, leaving just enough space for her eyes to see through. Sylvie had teamed it with a black dress that was close-fitting around the bodice but then it flared in a circle of voluminous tulle that whispered around her as she moved. She was channelling Cinderella on a bad mood day.

Everyone seemed to be there as couples or groups and Sylvie couldn't help feeling left on the outside.

Story of her life. It reminded her of when she had won a scholarship to a fee-paying school and how for weeks, months even, she hadn't fit in. She had to change her accent, work on her manners and control her acid tongue to finally make a handful of friends, none of whom she had contact with now. University had been a little better and her academic performance had garnered a level of respect that her birthplace and family lineage had not.

The master of ceremonies announced the opening of the ball and encouraged everyone to find a place to sit. As it was a masked ball, there was not a board outside the ballroom with nominated seating arrangements. The ball was designed to encourage people to mix, and try and guess who was sitting at their table. It was all part of the fun and games of the masked event.

Sylvie took a glass of champagne off a passing waiter and then made her way to a table right at the back of the room and was relieved to find it was far enough away from the podium to avoid being asked to draw out spot prizes or call any attention to herself. She took a sip of champagne, carefully lifting the lace of her mask to do so and surveyed the room, amazed at some of the masks people were wearing. She wondered what Jack would wear, if indeed he even showed up. He had probably decided his generous donation was enough, that turning up in person was unnecessary. Or maybe he had a hot date with one of his leggy blonde bombshells that took priority over a charity fundraiser ball.

The rest of the table filled up, all but the seat beside

her. Sylvie kept sipping at her champagne, more out of nervousness than thirst. God forbid that some narcissistic bore would sit next to her and proceed to tell her the story of his life. Why hadn't she thought to bring her mum? But this wasn't her mother's scene and besides, Sylvie was thirty-two years old and didn't need to hold her mum's hand to have a night out.

Finally, someone sat beside her and Sylvie couldn't explain the dip in her spirits when she saw it was an elderly man who seemed to be on his own. Why should she have hoped Jack might find her and sit beside her? She was behaving like a teenager with a crush on her favourite movie star.

Sylvie found herself scanning the room to see if she could pick out anyone she knew in the crowd, but there were hundreds of people, and she didn't feel like doing a circuit of the room to see if she could recognise anyone behind their mask.

Sylvie berated herself for her obsession with finding Jack in the crowd. What was she thinking? The last thing she wanted to do was draw attention to herself or to be seen talking to Jack if indeed he had come. She drank some more champagne and tried to identify some of her associates, solicitors, judges and interns she had worked with in the past but while some were easily identified in spite of their elaborate masks, she still found no sign of Jack. Then her eyes landed on someone that looked eerily like him. He was walking arm in arm with a beautiful brunette who was wearing a feathered mask a little like Sylvie's except it was white and silver.

'Jago Wilde, come over here and introduce me to your fiancée,' the old man sitting next to Sylvie called out over the noise of the music and chatter of the crowd.

So, this was Jack's middle brother, Jago. No wonder Sylvie had seen a likeness—the same handsome features and tall rangy frame, the sensual curve to his mouth, the slash of ink-black eyebrows, the dark hair and unusual blue eyes, although Jago's were a deep blue while Jack's were the colour of an Artic ice floe.

Jago introduced his fiancée, Mollie, to the gentleman and after exchanging a few brief words, he gently guided Mollie to a table towards the front of the ballroom.

The old man sitting next to Sylvie leaned closer to talk to her. 'You can pick a Wilde brother mask or no mask, eh? Handsome as the devil those three boys. Only one of them to settle down so far. I wonder who'll be next?'

Sylvie stretched her mouth into a tight smile. 'I'm sure it won't be Jack.'

The man's eyes took a keen interest in her, obviously trying to guess who she was. 'Do you know him personally?'

'Only professionally.'

'Ah, well, you'll know all about his reputation, then.'

'I do.'

Something in her tone made the old man peer a little more intensely at her. 'Don't let his reputation intimidate you. He's driven and fights hard to win but one day someone will teach him he can't have everything go his way.'

Sylvie tried to identify the old man who was in his mid to late eighties. His courtroom voice was vaguely familiar and although his mask covered most of his face, his grey hair was thick and plentiful. 'Are you by any chance Judge Cartleford?' she asked.

His eyes glinted. 'That I am, and you're Sylvia Rathbone. I always knew you'd do well for yourself.'

Sylvie smiled, almost bursting with pride that one of her favourite lecturers recognised her after all this time. 'Your lectures were the most entertaining of any I had at university.'

'That's kind of you but I'm fully retired now. I miss the students, bright and engaged ones like you most especially.' He let out a sigh and picked up his glass in a toast. 'But life goes on, eh? Let's toast your success.'

Sylvie clinked her glass against his and smiled. 'Thank you for your part in it.'

Judge Cartleford chuckled. 'You did it all yourself, Sylvie.'

'I don't know about that.'

'Don't be so modest,' Judge Cartleford said. 'But may I give you a word of advice?'

'Of course.'

He took a breath and then sighed. 'I lost my wife two years ago.'

'I'm so sorry.'

He gave her a sober look. 'I gave my life to law. I spent too many hours at work and neglected other areas of my life. I left the raising of our children to my wife, and I hardly see them now, they all live abroad. I only see my grandchildren if my son and daughter can be bothered to bring them to me as I'm too old to travel alone now. Law is competitive and all-consuming but don't let it take everything from you.'

Sylvie listened compassionately with a thread of worry weaving through her thoughts. Would she too look back on her life and wish she had done things differently?

'Thank you for sharing your wisdom,' she said. 'I'm still figuring out the work-life balance.'

Judge Cartleford glanced at her left hand. 'You're not married?'

Sylvie screwed up her mouth. 'Not even close. It's not something I've got on my list of things to do.'

'You can call me an old-fashioned old fool, but my advice is you can't give your whole life to your career. One day you'll retire and in a couple of years no one will even remember you.' There was a poignancy to his tone. Sylvie's eyes smarted with unshed tears for the old man's loneliness and regrets over how his life had played out and the choices he had made.

'I'm sure there are a lot of people out there who will never forget you,' Sylvie said. 'Me included.'

He patted her hand and smiled. 'That's very kind. Now, let's talk about more interesting things than my regrets.'

Their conversation veered into other less emotion-evoking areas, and Sylvie was glad of the old man's company, happy to talk to him about her house and garden and the cat she was trying to tame. And he chatted about his love of reading and the latest documentaries he had enjoyed. He eventually excused himself to shuffle off with his walking stick to seek out a colleague she had identified for him at a nearby table.

Sylvie sat, sipping at her glass of champagne, deep in reflective thought. But after a few minutes, some spidery sense told her Jack Wilde was in the room. There was a feathery sensation in her stomach, a prickle along her bare arms, her increased heart rate and pounding pulse told her he was not only nearby but searching for her in the crowd.

Jack arrived late to the ball after having to take a phone call from his grandfather who was in one of his obstreperous moods, complaining about the lack of contact from Jonas, the weather, the state of the country and a host of other things Jack had no power or interest in changing, except finding out where his youngest brother was and when he was coming home. He was even considering engaging a private investigator but knew Jonas would never forgive him if his cover was blown on a top-secret mission. Jack had somehow placated his grandfather enough to end the call on reasonably good terms, but it had made him forty minutes late for the fundraiser.

Jack stood at the ballroom door and took in the stunning decorations and the vast array of masked guests. It was like Carnevale in Venice, and he was pleased to see it was obviously such a success. A full house meant a lot of money would be raised for women's shelters and anger management programs for men who had a history of domestic violence.

Jack swept his gaze towards the back of the ballroom

as if some sort of internal radar had programmed him to do so. Even though Sylvie Rathbone was wearing a mask that covered her face, he knew it was her seated beside an elderly man who he recognised as a well-known retired judge, right at the back of the room. The old man shuffled to another table to greet someone, and Jack watched as Sylvie sipped champagne before freezing, as if she'd sensed his arrival. As she turned slowly towards Jack and met his gaze across the vast ballroom, something went *zzzzt* in his chest.

The band had assembled to play the first dance of the evening and Jack walked straight towards Sylvie, but, before he could get to her, another man from a nearby table rose and then after exchanging a few words with her, led her to the dance floor. The spike of jealousy that assailed Jack was both unexpected and painful. Him? Jealous? He had never had a moment of jealousy in his life. He never invested in a relationship with anyone long enough to evoke such an emotion. He frowned and turned to see his brother Jago approaching him with his fiancée, Mollie.

'Knew it was you as soon as I saw you,' Jago said, smiling behind his own mask. 'That Big Bad Wolf get-up really suits you.'

Jack had to force himself to act as nonchalantly as usual, but it took an effort. 'This old thing?' He forced a grin. 'I think I've worn it before. Hey, love the masks,' he addressed both Jago and Mollie. Jago was wearing a vampire mask and Mollie had a white feathery *Swan Lake* vibe to hers.

'Did you just get here?' Mollie asked.

'Yeah, Maxwell phoned and I had to listen to him get a few things off his chest before I could hang up. Have either of you heard from Jonas yet? That seems to be Maxwell's biggest grief right now, mine too, to be honest.'

'Ours too,' Jago said, pulling Mollie close to his side. 'We can't make any arrangements for the wedding until we know when he's coming home. If he doesn't contact us soon, we're going to go ahead and get married without him there.'

'It would break Gran's heart to not have the family together for such an important occasion,' Jack said. 'You know how sentimental she is.'

'I know but this is the longest he's ever been away. It's hard not to worry something might be wrong,' Jago said, with an undercurrent of concern in his tone.

'I hear you,' Jack said, sighing. 'Let's give it another couple of weeks and if we haven't heard anything, we'll have to take decisive action to track him down.'

'A private investigator?' Jago asked.

'It's one option.' Jack's tone was grim. 'The other is to wait it out and hope his work is done and he comes home soon.'

'It's been eight months,' Jago said. 'The longest he's been away before is six.'

'I know,' Jack said. 'But some projects take longer than others and this must be an important one for him to block all of us from contacting him, including Tessa. I thought he was getting serious with her so I was surprised when he enlisted me to break things off on his behalf.'

'So did I. Have you heard from her again?' Jago asked. 'We were hoping to get her to do our wedding cake again but her shop in Notting Hill closed down. She's now working from home, but her website says she isn't taking on any work for a month or two.'

'I blocked her on my phone,' Jack said with a tiny twinge of guilt. 'I have enough on my plate without having to console Jonas's ex.' He cast his eyes towards the dance floor and saw an opportunity to join in the current dance. 'Excuse me, I have something to do.'

Sylvie was about to move to the new partner in the line when Jack Wilde cut in with a confident, 'May I?' to the middle-aged man with whom she was about to dance.

'Be my guest,' the man said and disappeared into the ballroom crowd.

Sylvie knew it was Jack even before his arms came around her. Her sensual radar had sensed his presence the moment he entered the ballroom. He was wearing a wolf mask that gave him an even more dangerous air than he already possessed. Her flesh shivered with awareness as soon as Jack's arms went around her body in the waltz position. Her hand was almost swallowed by the broadness of his and her heart thudded in excitement and her pulse raced with hectic speed. The steel band of his arm around her waist seared her skin and the closeness of his hard male body sent her senses reeling. Never had she been more aware of her body, the way it so neatly moulded against his in spite of their differences in height.

'I've been wanting to do this all night,' Jack said, smiling down at her.

'What? Dance?'

'Hold you in my arms.'

Sylvie's eyebrows rose. 'But you only arrived a few minutes ago.'

He grinned down at her, his blue eyes glittering through his mask. 'You were waiting for me?'

She gave him a haughty stare, which was quite a feat with his body sending hers into a tailspin of delight as he whirled her out of the dance line and towards an exit. 'Of course not. Hey, where are you taking me?'

'Somewhere I can talk to you in private.' He released her, took her by the hand and led her out of the ballroom to a balcony outside that overlooked the city. It was an unusually warm evening for early summer and Sylvie wondered if it wasn't the outside temperature heating her but Jack Wilde's firm, gentle grip on her hand.

'How did you recognise me so easily?' His mask almost entirely covered his face but she could see his glinting smile, his white teeth starkly contrasted by his dark mask.

'You have an aura of arrogance that no mask could ever disguise,' Sylvie said. 'What if I wanted to dance with that man?'

'Did you?' His eyes burned into hers and a tiny shiver tingled down her spine.

'No. He had sweaty hands and bad breath.'

Jack laughed and pulled her back into a waltz, dancing with her on the balcony with the glittering lights of the city shimmering like fairy lights.

'Do you think this is wise?' Sylvie asked.

'What? Us dancing?'

'Us doing anything together.' She could feel her cheeks heating and kept her head down. The loaded meaning to her words seemed to echo in the silence.

Jack stopped dancing but still maintained his hold of her. And Sylvie stayed there, relishing in the warm band of his arm at her back, and his hand holding hers. 'We're colleagues dancing at a fundraising ball. I don't see a problem with that,' he said.

Sylvie sensed him looking down at her and slowly raised her gaze back to his. 'Why are you doing this?'

'What am I doing?'

She ran the tip of her tongue over her lips, aware of the dark gleam of his eyes following the movement. The air tightened, crackling with tension like a current of electricity passing between their bodies. Her gaze went to his mouth and her body moved closer to him, drawn by a magnetic force field she had no power to resist. Jack moved at the same time, his head bent, his eyes hooded, his warm mint-scented breath caressing her upturned mouth.

'You're not going to kiss me, are you?' Her voice was supposed to come out tart and reproving but it was barely more than a breathless whisper.

'That would depend.'

'On what?'

His mouth moved infinitesimally closer. 'On whether you want me to.'

Sylvie inched closer, drawn to him as if she had no say in the matter. 'Do you want to kiss me?' The words were out and in a breathless, almost hopeful tone that she knew was reflected in her gaze.

He tipped up her chin with his index finger, locking his eyes on hers. 'I admit I want to kiss you, but I wouldn't do anything you wouldn't agree to.'

Her eyes moved between each of his, trying to make him out. Was he playing with her? Toying with her? Seeing how far he could go, or was he being serious for once? She was usually a good judge of character but somehow with Jack she was thrown into a whirlpool of confusion. Or maybe that was because it was her who was sending him mixed signals. She bit her lip and gently eased out of his hold, smoothing her hands down the voluminous tulle skirt of her dress. 'How do I know if this is just a game you're playing?'

'What do you mean?'

'I get the feeling you see me as a challenge. A conquest to add to your long list of conquests.'

'I'm attracted to you. Very attracted.' His eyes glittered and he added in a husky tone, 'We moved so well together when dancing it made me think how hot it would be—'

'Stop.' Sylvie put her index finger over his lips to stall his speech. Her finger tingled as her skin came in contact with the raspy dark shadow of stubble around and below his mouth.

He placed his hand over hers and gently eased it away from his mouth, holding it within the cage of his. 'You say that with your lips but not with your eyes. I can see how much you want me. I could feel it when we were dancing together.'

'It's your imagination. Your overblown ego makes you think there isn't a woman alive who wouldn't fall into bed with you.' Sylvie tried to keep her eyes away from his mouth but she felt an irresistible pull that no amount of willpower could withstand.

'You're doing it again.'

'What am I doing?'

'You're looking at my mouth.'

'Is that a crime?' Sylvie asked. 'What if I was checking if you had parsley in your teeth?'

His rich deep chuckle of amusement sent a shiver rolling down her spine. 'Do I?'

'No.'

'Are you here with a partner?' Jack asked.

'No, I came by myself.'

'Me too.'

Sylvie raised her eyebrows in surprise. 'What? No leggy blonde supermodels available for you this evening? My heart bleeds.'

Jack gave a chuckle and leaned indolently against the balustrade, watching her with amusement through his wolf mask. 'I'm hoping my luck will change by the end of the evening.'

'I'd better go back inside…' She took three steps before his deep voice stopped her.

'Sylvie?'

She turned to look at him standing in the shadows of the balcony, his mask concealing his expression. 'Yes?'

'Save the last dance for me.' It wasn't a request but a

statement of command, and though she wanted to say no—knew she should say no—she somehow couldn't find the willpower to do it. She wanted to feel his arms around her once more. She wanted to be held close against his firm body and feel the stirring of his blood against her. And foolish as it was, she wanted to feel his sensual-looking mouth on hers. It was like she was under some sort of spell; some superpower was commanding her to do things she would never normally do, not with her arch-enemy Jack Wilde.

Sylvie left him on the balcony without giving him a reply.

Jack was about to go back into the ballroom when he felt the vibration of his phone in his jacket pocket. He reached for it and glanced at the screen to decide whether or not to answer it. His eyes widened as he saw his brother Jonas's name, and relief flooded through him in a rush that made him feel light-headed. 'Jonas? Where the hell have you been? We've been trying to contact you for months.'

'Sorry, but I had important business to see to. I told you I'd be in contact as soon as I could.'

'Surely you could've pinged us an email or something from time to time,' Jack said. 'I had to cover for you for Gran's birthday. She had a fall a couple of weeks before. She could have died and you'd only be finding out about it now.'

'Is she okay?' A note of concern rang in Jonas's voice.

'More than okay. She's ecstatic about Jago and Mollie getting married as soon as you get back to be a groomsman.'

'Jago and Mollie? But I thought—'

'It's a long story but they got back together and are desperate to get married. I'll leave it to Jago to explain it all. When will you be back?'

'I just have a few loose ends to sort out here and I'll be home. Early July at the latest.'

Jack blew out a long breath, releasing months of tension he had got so used to holding in his body over his brother's absence, that he felt almost limbless without it. 'Have you told Maxwell and Gran?'

'I'll call them tomorrow. It's a bit late now, they'll be in bed, or at least Gran will.'

Jack turned to look at the view of London at night. There was too much light pollution to see anything but three or four stars. 'Mate, I was really worried about you. I was about to hire a private investigator to track you down.' Jack didn't bother disguising the gravitas in his tone.

There was a lengthy silence.

Jonas released a whooshing breath. 'Yeah, I guess you would've been but I can't always reveal my whereabouts when I'm away. This was a serious project. More serious than anything I've faced before.'

'You didn't even send Gran a birthday card.'

Another silence.

'I'll make it up to her,' Jonas said.

'Can you talk about your mission?' Jack asked.

'No, not yet. When I get home, okay?'

'Fine. But you'd better call Jago and give him a

firm return date so he and Mollie can get their wedding plans under way.'

'What about you, Jack? Have you acquired any plans to settle down since I've been away?'

Jack gave a laugh that sounded slightly off-key. 'You know me. Footloose and fancy-free, although I've finally moved into my new house.'

'I'll look forward to seeing it.'

'Safe travels, man.'

'Thanks. See you soon.'

Jack slipped his phone back in his pocket and headed back inside the ballroom to find Sylvie. The revelry had kicked up a notch and the dancing had moved from ballads to rock and roll. He searched the dance floor and the tables but he couldn't find Sylvie anywhere. He waited another half an hour in case she had gone to the bathroom or met up with a friend or colleague and was chatting somewhere, but eventually he had to accept she wasn't there.

Cinderella had left the ball and he hadn't even seen her go.

The acute sense of disappointment that assailed him was both unexpected and deeply unsettling. Ever since he had danced with her, he had longed to do it again. He could still feel her petite form in his arms, moving across the dance floor in perfect time with him. He had wanted to kiss her outside on the balcony but while he sensed her attraction to him, he knew she was holding him at bay due to his playboy reputation.

A young women wearing a Cleopatra mask and gold

close-fitting dress shimmied over to him, holding out her hand. 'Hey, handsome. Come and dance with me.'

Jack gave a smile that made his face ache. 'Sorry, but I have to leave.' He didn't wait for the woman's reply, simply turned and walked out of the nearest exit.

CHAPTER SIX

SYLVIE LEFT THE ball early, which was cowardly of her, but one dance with Jack Wilde had shown her she was in danger of losing her head over him. As it was, she had recreated in her mind every step of that dance with him, remembering how it felt to have his arms hold her close, how it felt to have him take the lead with confidence, turning her with ease. And she remembered every moment of their time on the balcony, how his eyes kept following her every movement. Would he have kissed her if she'd agreed to it? She ran her tongue over her lips and imagined how his mouth would feel pressed on hers. She hadn't been kissed in months, that was why she was fantasising about Jack. What other explanation could there be? She didn't even like him.

Well, maybe that was a little white lie. There were things about him she did admire, for instance his generosity towards the fundraising ball and the fact he insisted on doing it anonymously. If he was as arrogant and prideful as she had imagined, surely he would be making sure people knew about every pound he donated?

She was starting to see Jack was a little more complicated than he wanted people to believe. He played the laid-back charming playboy role so well, he laughed and joked his way through life, and yet there were sides to him he didn't want people to know about. It made her all the more determined to uncover them, even if it meant she'd have to inch closer to him than she would normally do.

Once she got home, Sylvie carefully packed away her Venetian mask and changed out of her evening dress, hanging it on a padded hanger on the door of her wardrobe. She took off her make-up, and slipped on a nightgown and wrap, tying it loosely around her waist. She went to her bedroom window, which overlooked her back garden as well as Jack's. She found herself looking towards his house, wondering what time he would come home from the ball. Maybe he wouldn't come home at all. Maybe he'd stay overnight in his brother's fancy hotel with one of the beautiful women he had met at the event.

Sylvie glanced towards his house and her eyes rounded in surprise to see him in his smartly decorated kitchen downstairs, which was partially visible from her upstairs bedroom. He had taken off his mask and loosened his bow tie—it hung undone around his neck as if he couldn't be bothered taking it off. He removed his jacket and she watched as he draped it over a kitchen bar-stool. She moved back a fraction behind her curtain to keep out of his line of vision and watched as he unlocked his back door and stepped outside.

The sensor light came on like a stage light, showcasing him like the leading star in a one-man performance. He was standing with his hands on his hips, his gaze directed towards the back of his garden. Not that it was much of a garden as yet, more like a mud pile, but at least it was fenced on all sides. He turned and went back inside and disappeared from her line of vision for a moment or two.

Sylvie told herself she should stop staring and go to bed but, somehow, she stayed, watching out of her bedroom window, transfixed by Jack's every movement. Had he brought someone home with him? Her heart gave a thump and she peered around the edge of her curtain to see if anyone was with him.

He appeared once more and Sylvie held her breath, but this time he was carrying something in one hand. She narrowed her gaze, trying to figure out what it was. He stepped out into the range of the sensor light again, bent down and placed what looked like a square foil packet of cat food on the top step. He straightened and, stepping back a few paces, paused for a long moment, his gaze concentrated on the shadows. Sylvie flattened her back against her bedroom wall, counting to three before she peered around the curtain but when she looked, he was gone. Then, four more seconds later, his sensor light turned off and the back of his property was enveloped in darkness.

A couple of evenings later, Sylvie was out in her garden, watering her pots when her mother called on the phone. 'Darling,' her mother said in an excited tone Sylvie barely recognised as belonging to the usually low-in-spirits woman, 'I have something important to tell you.'

'What is it?' Sylvie found herself holding her breath in the loaded silence before her mother answered.

'I'm seeing someone.'

'What? A psychologist?' Sylvie asked, glad her advice had finally been taken after all these years. Her mother was a very private person and had always refused to speak to a health professional about her loneliness and feelings of rejection post-divorce.

'No, not a psychologist, a retired vet,' her mother said with a girlish giggle. 'We're dating.'

'*Dating?*' Sylvie shrieked in shock.

Her mother laughed and that was another thing Sylvie wasn't used to hearing—her mum sounding blissfully, deliriously happy. 'I can't wait to introduce Patrick to you. He's the most wonderful man. He treats me like a princess and is so generous and—'

'Are you sure he's not love-bombing you like Dad did all those years ago?' Sylvie was terrified history was repeating itself. She knew a lot about toxic relationships through her work. Some people fell into the same trap with a subsequent relationship, often without realising it as they were so caught up in the heady feeling of being 'loved,' when what was really happening was manipulation and coercive control in its early stages.

'Darling, he's not doing any such thing,' her mother answered. 'We met at the garden centre café. I'd seen him a few times before but we never really spoke. But a couple of months ago, he helped me carry some compost to the car and we got talking. He was happily married for thirty-seven years but his wife died five years ago and he's lonely and, well, I told him a little about myself and then we met for coffee and things went from there.'

Sylvie was lost for words. On one hand she was delighted for her mother, but on the other the cynical part of her worried that her mother would be hurt all over again. 'How long have you been seeing him?'

'Eight weeks and three days.'

Sylvie absently watered another section of the garden with the hose, still unable to believe her mother had finally found happiness, but also wary of what heartbreak could be ahead and how Sylvie would have to pick up the pieces as she had all those years ago. 'How serious are you about him?'

'If you're asking if I'm sleeping with him then—'

'You don't have to tell me that,' Sylvie quickly interjected. How ironic that her mother was now having regular sex while she could barely recall the last time she had slept with anyone. 'I'm happy if you're happy but I can't help being worried about you.'

'I appreciate your concern, darling, but I have to move on with my life. I've wasted too much of it as it is. I'm enjoying being with Patrick and once you meet him, you'll see he's nothing like your father. He's kind and gentle and supportive and he makes me laugh.'

Sylvie couldn't stop recalling Jack Wilde's attractive smile and his sharp wit. 'Yes, well, a sense of humour is a good quality in anyone, I guess.'

'I'll text you some possible dates for a dinner at

your place because we're coming up to London for a weekend soon. I'll bring the main course if you make dessert. Just a shop one will do—I know you're busy. Oh, and you can invite a partner if you like. Are you seeing anyone?'

Sylvie's gaze drifted to the house next door and an invisible moth fluttered its wings in her stomach. 'No one in particular.'

'Don't be like me, darling, and waste years of your life thinking all men are creeps. There are good men out there, you just have to be brave enough to take a chance on someone who captures your attention.'

Sylvie ended the call a few minutes later, still reeling from her mother's news. She pointed the hose at another section of the garden, keeping an eye out for Shadow, who hadn't yet eaten the food Sylvie had put out for her earlier. She hadn't seen the little cat for a couple of days and was beginning to get worried. What if she had been run over or was lying somewhere injured and afraid? Her mind was so preoccupied with her worries over the cat and her mother's news that she didn't register she had company.

'Howdy, neighbour.' Jack's deep voice made her jump and she turned to face the fence but forgot she had the hose in her hand. The water hit Jack straight in the face and he yelped and stepped out of its spray, shaking his head like a dog who had just had a bath.

Sylvie dropped the hose but it coiled and twisted like an angry snake, shooting water in all directions. She dashed over to the tap and turned it off and then went over to the fence to apologise. 'I'm so sorry, that wasn't intentional. I was distracted by a phone call.'

Jack brushed his hair back from his face, a grin making his eyes crinkle attractively at the corners and those gorgeous dimples to appear. 'Your apology isn't accepted unless you join me in a drink. I've finally got my house in order. Want to take a look?'

How could she say no? Especially when she didn't want to say no. She wanted to see inside Jack's house, and she wanted to be in his company.

A short time later, Jack opened his front door to her. His dark hair was still damp and she grimaced at him. 'I'm really sorry about the shower I gave you.'

A devilish gleam came into his eyes. 'I like nothing more than a water fight.' He closed the door once she was inside and added, 'Down at Wildewood, my family's estate, my brothers and I would have them in the holidays on the rare occasions we were there altogether.'

Sylvie looked up at him in surprise. 'Didn't you spend the holidays together?'

'Christmas and Easter were spent at home. But my grandfather sent us to various camps during the summer holidays. He said it was to make it less tiring for my grandmother as entertaining three energetic boys all at once was a handful.'

'Are you close to your brothers?'

He hesitated for a nanosecond as if thinking about it. 'Not as much as we should be. My youngest brother hasn't been home in eight months. We've had zero contact with him but he finally rang me at the ball. I was about to engage the services of a private investigator to track him down.'

'You're making me glad I'm an only child,' Sylvie said. 'I only have my mother to worry about.' She bit her lip and then added, 'That's kind of why I hosed you. I just found out my mother is seeing someone after twenty-two years of being single.'

Jack's eyebrows lifted. 'Twenty-two years is a long time to be celibate.'

'Yes…'

There was a small silence.

'Hey, I'm forgetting why you're here. Come on. I'll give you the grand tour.'

Sylvie followed him as he showed her the beautiful renovation of his house. The layout was similar to hers and his taste, to her surprise, was not dissimilar to hers either. Clean lines, lots of light, an open-plan kitchen and living spaces, three bedrooms, a study and an entertainment room, and two gorgeously appointed bathrooms. The furniture was a mix of modern and antique, giving the house a sophisticated yet modern feel. The only difference was Jack had turned one of the bedrooms into a gym.

'You have good taste,' Sylvie said.

'I can't take the credit for all this.' Jack waved his hand to encompass their surroundings. 'I hired an interior decorator.'

'Still, they usually consult with the client about their preferences.'

'True but I gave him pretty free rein.' Jack opened the fridge and took out a bottle of wine. 'Drink?'

'Sure.'

He poured two glasses of wine and came over to hand her one. She took it from him but the brush of his fingers sent a crackle of electricity through her body. His eyes met hers and he held his glass up. 'What shall we drink to?'

'Erm…' She was lost for words, mesmerised by the blue of his eyes and the intensity of them as they held hers.

'How about to friends, not enemies?' he suggested with a glint in his eyes.

'Okay. Friends not enemies.' She clinked her glass against his, wondering if she were mad to make such a toast. Why was she allowing herself to be drawn to him when she didn't like him. *You do like him. You like him a lot.* The voice inside her head pointed out. Maybe her mother and Judge Cartleford were right—it was time for her to live a little before life passed her by. But Sylvie was a professional, a rule follower, a person who coloured between the lines. Even thinking about a fling with Jack made her feel as if she was stepping over a boundary, treading on forbidden territory. Dangerous territory.

They each took a sip of wine, their movements almost in unison. Then Jack put his glass down on the kitchen counter. 'I've been thinking about the other night.'

'The ball?'

He smiled and took the wine glass out of her hand and turned away to set it on the counter beside his.

Then he faced her again, holding out his hands. 'Shall we dance?'

'What, now?'

'Why not?'

'Don't we need music?'

Jack spoke to his automated system and a slow-moving ballad began playing. She found herself putting her hands in his and did nothing to stop him drawing her closer to his body. His arms came around her and he guided her in a waltz that was sexy and smooth and sensual, their bodies moving as one. Sylvie had never considered herself a particularly competent dancer. She had never taken lessons and usually avoided dancing at weddings and parties. But with Jack's arms around her, guiding her, leading her, she felt like she was dancing on a cloud.

It made her wonder—not for the first time—what it would be like in his arms, making love with him. Her body craved his touch more and more. It was as if their first dance at the ball had set off a need in her she hadn't realised she possessed—the need to be held and pleasured by Jack Wilde. Were her feelings of lust masquerading as dislike? Had she put up walls because she knew instinctively that he could unlock her sensuality and take it to heights it had never been before?

But how could she maintain her professional distance if she slept with him? How could she stop herself wanting more than he was prepared to give? She couldn't stop fantasising about him kissing her, touching her, pleasuring her until she saw stars. But how could she allow herself to relax her boundaries? Especially with Jack Wilde?

'I like how you move with me,' he said, holding her closer.

'I usually have two left feet but you're good at taking the lead.'

He brought one hand up to cup her cheek, his thumb stroking back and forth across her skin, his eyes locked on hers. 'Now, about that kiss.' His voice was low and gravelly.

'What kiss?' Was that her voice? That whispery soft breath of air that had heady anticipation threaded through it.

'This kiss,' he said, and lowered his mouth to hers.

Sylvie leaned into his kiss, delighting in the rush of adrenaline as his lips moved against hers, gently at first, as soft as down feather but then, a flame was lit and heat and fire blazed between their mouths. Her blood pounded through her veins, her heart hammered against her breastbone and her desire roared like an inferno. She was out of control and was glad of it. She had never felt such a ferocious rush of desire.

It was magic, black magic that cast a spell over her, making her hungry for more of his touch. Her heart rate was so high it was clearly trying to get into the *Guinness Book of World Records*. She breathed in the subtle but intoxicating lime and lemongrass notes of Jack's aftershave and something else that was one part musk and three parts male. Desire moved through her body like a prowling hungry beast looking for satiation. Never had she wanted a man more than this man.

Was it because he was her enemy in a legal case? Was it because she was crossing a boundary she had sworn she would never cross? Or was it simply because Jack Wilde was irresistible?

But if she slept with him, she could potentially be compromising her professional status as a solicitor who advocated for her female clients. She had worked so hard to build her brand and reputation. What if her involvement with Jack was discovered and destroyed her reputation? There were no rules about lawyers on opposing sides being friends or lovers, but Sylvie had her own rules, and they did not include fraternising with London's most flagrant playboy. If she agreed to a fling, it would have to be on her terms. A one-night thing just to keep her reputation safe.

Jack's tongue slipped between her lips and a shock wave went through her body, making her feel as if someone had shuffled a deck of cards in her belly. Quickly. Vegas-card-table quickly. Need crawled through her flesh, sending tingles to her breasts, the slightly prickling sensation of them shifting against the lace of her bra as if they couldn't wait for Jack to place his hands or mouth on them. Her inner core contracted, pulsed, throbbed for his intimate possession.

Every time Jack's tongue touched hers a dart of lust speared her between the legs. Desire moved through her body in tingling waves, making her aware of her erogenous zones as if it were the first time they'd ever been activated. His mouth continued its passionate exploration of hers, his tongue making love with hers until she was making whimpering sounds of delight and encouragement.

His stubble grazed her face as he changed position, a deep groan coming from inside his throat as if he too was being swept away by the flashpoint of lust that had exploded between them. One of his hands splayed its fingers through her hair as he held her in an achingly tender embrace. A part of her mind reminded her he was a practised playboy who knew all the moves to make a woman crazy for him, but another part of her wanted to believe his tenderness, that his passion was only for her.

After a long, breathless interval, Jack eased back away from her mouth and looked down at her with lust-glazed eyes. 'Is that as far as this goes?'

Sylvie was so shaken by his kiss, sensually rattled by his caressing mouth, that she found it hard to find her voice. 'I… I… Do you want more?' She wanted more. Way more. It was liberating to admit it to herself even though her rule-following nature rang warning bells. But wasn't that part of Jack's allure to her? He was forbidden fruit and she was tempted beyond her measure of self-control.

'That must be more than obvious.'

She was standing so close to him she could feel how much he wanted her. But Sylvie didn't want him to think she was interested in anything but a fling because she wasn't. She wasn't waiting for the white wedding and the pram and the picket fence future. She was a career woman with her own legal practice. She had no time for the fairy tale, only her clients. And yet…

there was something missing from her life and it was this—sex. No-strings sex. Fun sex. Exciting, flesh-tingling sex.

Sylvie looked up at him, her heart still pounding from his spine-tingling kiss. 'How much more? Are we talking a one-nighter? Because that's all I'd want. A one-off to scratch the itch.'

Jack's eyes widened a fraction and his smile seemed a little off-kilter. 'One night? That's all?'

'Sure. I'm not the fairy tale type, Jack. I'm more like you than you probably realise. I don't have time for relationships, just the odd fling.'

There was a questioning frown on his forehead. 'When was your last one?'

Sylvie gave a self-deprecating grimace. 'Six months ago.'

'Why so long?'

She shrugged one shoulder. 'I got a little tired of online dating. Thought I'd take a break to concentrate on work.'

His hands came to rest on her hips, bringing her even closer to his hot, hard warmth. 'Why did you leave the ball before we had another dance?'

'I was still a bit undecided about you.'

He hooked one eyebrow upwards. 'What changed your mind?'

Sylvie decided to be honest. 'Dancing with you turned me on. It made me realise I should live a little on the wild side.'

Jack stroked a slow hand down the length of her spine, sending sparks of delight straight to her core.

'You and me too, baby. One dance wasn't enough.' He lowered his head and nuzzled his mouth against the sensitive skin of her neck, just below her ear. 'You left me hungry for more.'

His voice was a low growl of need that thrilled her into a shiver of delightful anticipation. His lips moved from her neck and came back to her mouth, sealing it with the heat and potency of his. Their tongues duelled in a sexy tango that made her knees loosen with increasing desire.

He walked her backwards towards the nearest wall, then placed one hand on the wall beside her head and continued his ravishing kiss. Sylvie responded with more fervour than she had ever felt before, locking her arms around his neck, her fingers toying with his thick dark wavy hair. Something about his mouth—the taste, the texture, the skill—sent her senses into overdrive.

His lower body was close enough for her to feel what she was doing to him and it ramped up her need for him all the more. The hard heat of him pushing against her made her almost crazy with lust. Nothing mattered but getting naked with him. She pulled his shirt out of his trousers and ran her hands over his warm, muscular chest. He groaned as if her touch pleased him, so she became bolder and moved her hands to stroke and caress his back and shoulders.

Jack reached for the zipper at the back of her dress, pausing briefly to ask, 'Are you sure this is what you want?'

'Never surer.' Sylvie wondered how she could even talk when her breathing was so hectic with excitement and anticipation. His skin was hot and smooth under the caress of her hands, his muscles toned with hard exercise. She couldn't wait to explore him in intimate detail, to freeze-frame the memory of him for future fantasies.

Jack ran her zipper down to the base of her spine, then stroked her back the way she had stroked his—slowly, sensually, exploratively. She shivered under his touch, his broad hands so warm and erotic as they moved over every exposed inch of her. Then he slipped his hand under her black lacy knickers and cupped her bottom, a deep groan sounding at the back of his throat. 'I love the feel of you. Your skin is like silk.'

Sylvie had to stand on tiptoe to link her arms around his neck, her breasts pushing against his chest and her pelvis on fire.

'Let's take this upstairs,' he said. 'I don't want to shock the neighbours.'

'I'm the only neighbour who can see you,' Sylvie pointed out.

Jack grinned down at her. 'So you are, but still, a bed is more comfortable than the floor and I don't want our first time to be up against the wall.' He gave her a gleaming look and added, 'I want to take my time with you.'

Sylvie shuddered in anticipation, and he took her by the hand and led her upstairs to his bedroom. There wasn't time to take in anything but the king-sized bed that dominated the room. Jack removed his shirt, tossing it to a chair in the corner, then helped her out of her dress. He stood looking at her in her bra and knickers, his eyes glinting with lust.

'Every part of you is so damn beautiful.'

Sylvie didn't want to think how many times he had said the very same thing to numerous other women. Tonight was about her and him alone. Exploring the chemistry she had been trying to ignore since the day she met him. His confidence and his arrogance had annoyed her, but nothing about his kisses or his touch did. They mesmerized her, enchanted her, bewitched her.

Finally, they were both naked and Jack laid her down on the bed, leaning over her, with one hand beside her head, his knee bent on the mattress. It gave her easy access to his erection and she circled his swollen length with her fingers and relished in his groans of pleasure. His mouth crushed hers, his kiss passionate, urgent, his tongue flicking against hers, calling it into erotic play.

He pulled away from her mouth to move down her body, taking his time over each of her breasts, exploring them, circling each nipple with his tongue, sucking, stroking, teasing until, overcome with sensual pleasure, she was writhing and arching her back like a cat.

She sucked in a breath as he moved lower, dipping the tip of his tongue into the tiny cave of her belly button. No one had ever caressed her there without her pulling away in embarrassment, so she'd had no idea how many nerve endings were waiting there to be activated. Her breath all but stalled when he went lower to her most feminine part of her body.

It wasn't her first time that someone had tried to pleasure her there but this time was completely different. Firstly, she didn't tense up and squirm with embarrassment. Secondly, the moment Jack's lips and tongue separated her female flesh, she could feel the tremors of pleasure building in the network of sensitive nerves throughout her pelvis.

He seemed to know exactly where and how long to caress her to send her out of her mind with an intense orgasm that shuddered and shook through her body. A giant wave captured her, spun her around and around, washing over her in ripples of heat and fizzing sensations like the froth of expensive champagne. Finally, the wave subsided and she was left spent and breathless, looking up at him with a dazed expression.

'Oh wow…' She could barely speak, could barely believe her body could respond so violently, so intensely, so pleasurably.

Jack pressed a firm kiss to her mouth and she tasted herself on his lips—another erotic moment she had not experienced before. 'I need to get a condom.' He moved off the bed to source a condom in the en suite, then came back and sheathed himself before joining her again on the bed. The glinting light of anticipation in his eyes made her want him all over again.

A troubling thought entered her mind—what if this one night wasn't enough? What if making love with him this one time only fuelled her desire all the more? What if her hunger for him could not be satiated by a one-off encounter? But then, he wasn't a relationships guy any more than she was a relationships woman. They were practically equal on that score, except she had undoubtably had far fewer lovers than he.

Jack lay over her, resting his weight on his elbows, looking deep into her eyes. 'Everything still okay?'

She smiled and linked her arms around his trim waist. 'Of course. Why wouldn't it be? You just gave me the best orgasm of my life.'

His smile made his eyes light up but this time she didn't read it as arrogance or pride. 'I'm glad because one-sided sex is no fun for anyone.'

'I've had more than my fair share of one-sided sex, unfortunately.' Sylvie wasn't sure why she had told him such an intimate detail about her life. What would he care?

Jack frowned. 'Is that why you gave up on dating for six months?'

She lifted her hand to his face and traced the square line of his stubbly jaw. 'More or less.'

'So, will you go back to it after this?'

Sylvie gave a loose shrug. 'I can't have my mother having more sex than me, now can I?' Her smile was rueful. 'I'll see what time allows. Work is so all-consuming that I don't have much time for anything other than short-term flings.'

'You sound like me.' He said it lightly but there was a frown lurking around his eyes.

'As the eldest Wilde brother, aren't you meant to settle down at some point and produce a couple of heirs?'

Jack grimaced. 'Jago is pretty keen to have a family with Mollie. I'll hand that responsibility to him.'

Sylvie stroked the curvature of his mouth, delighting in the feel of his stubble as it caught against her skin. He captured her finger and sucked on it, his eyes holding hers in an erotically charged lock.

He released her finger and smiled down at her. 'I have some unfinished business with you.'

Sylvie gave an involuntary shiver at the intense look in his blue eyes. 'Since this is going to be the one and only time, you'd better make the most of it.' She kept her tone light and playful but deep down she was already regretting putting such a short time frame on their involvement…and yet, he would have if she hadn't, so she had thought it best to get in first.

Jack's expression barely changed but something told her he was not used to having lovers setting the limits on being with him. His mouth came back to hers in a firm kiss that spoke of his growing need. She stroked his length again and again, listening as his breathing became more erratic with every glide of her hand against his swollen erection.

He moved her hand off him so he could access her body, taking his time to caress her until she was swollen and wet. Her need for him was a burning ache that drove every other thought out of her head. She writhed beneath him, desperate to feel him inside her, restless to feel the ultimate fulfillment of physical union.

Finally, he drove into her with a deep guttural groan of pleasure, his movements slow at first but then gradually increasing. His sounds of pleasure made her skin come up in a spray of delicate goose bumps. Her senses were reeling from the feel of him moving inside her, faster, deeper, more urgently, each movement causing a delicious friction that triggered all her nerve endings. She arched her spine to get more contact where she needed it, her body straining, swelling and quivering with the need to fly off to the stratosphere again.

Jack slipped his hand down between their rocking bodies, giving her that extra bit of friction that sent her flying into ecstasy. Her body shook with the power of it as each delicious ripple turned into an earthquake and she split into a thousand pieces. She lost all sense of thought and reason. She was spinning in a wild vortex of sensations that surpassed anything she had ever experienced before. The sexy glide of his hard body, the slick of their sweat, the scent of their lovemaking, the sounds they were both making were so intimate and erotic, and she knew she would never forget this experience.

Jack waited until her orgasm was subsiding before he took his own. She felt him tense all over, his momentary pause heralding his point of no return. She enjoyed the feeling of him losing control, the deep thrusts of his body, the shudders, the groans, the gasps of his breathing trying to return to normal in the aftermath.

Jack stayed on top of her, his head buried beside her neck. 'I can't move.' His voice was muffled and his breath tickled the sensitive skin of her nape.

Sylvie stroked her hands up and down his back and shoulders and then even lower to his taut buttocks. 'This is the part where I never usually know what to say. But in this case, I can say thank you for showing me how good sex can be.'

Jack rolled away to deal with the condom and then came back to lie on his side with his head propped on one hand to look at her. His other hand stroked her body from breast to belly and back again, each movement slow and sensual, sending delicious tingles through her body all over again. 'Are you saying it's not always good for you?' There was a pleated frown between his eyes.

Sylvie turned on her side and ran her hand up and down his muscular thigh. 'The problem with casual sex, for women at least, is it isn't always guaranteed it will be mutually satisfying. Sometimes…most times…the chemistry isn't right. Or it's too soon or I'm not attracted to the person other than physically. It's complicated.'

Jack's hand glided up to caress the curve of her cheek and she found it hard not to purr like a cat. His touch was both electrifying and tender as the brush of a feather. No wonder he was such a successful playboy. He could make a nun cast aside her vows with just a look. 'I've been thinking…' He left the sentence hanging as if he was indeed still thinking something through. There was a faint frown on his brow showing a serious side to his thoughts.

'About?'

'Never mind.' He gave his signature grin and leaned down to press a brief firm kiss to her mouth. 'Do you fancy a nightcap before you go home?'

'Just a quick one.' Sylvie told herself she wasn't disappointed he hadn't asked her to stay overnight. Why would he? She lived next door. She was perfectly safe walking a few steps to her own home. But even so, a ripple of disappointment ran through her. This was it.

The one-night stand was over. The one-night stand *she* had suggested.

There was no point in wanting more from Jack Wilde. Everyone knew he was the Playboy Prince of the Pick-up. The One-Night-Wonder Lover. The No-Strings Sex God.

Was there any woman in the world who could make him change? No, people only changed if they wanted to, if they saw the need to change. And nothing about Jack suggested he was at that point in life where he was no longer happy with the status quo.

Sylvie had to content herself that in sleeping with him, she had just done what she had sworn she would never do—join the long list of Jack Wilde's lovers.

CHAPTER SEVEN

Jack returned home after walking Sylvie back to her house. She, of course, insisted she was perfectly capable of finding her own way home, but he wouldn't take no for an answer. He said good-night, she shut the door and he walked back to his place with his thoughts as messy as tangled fishing line. So, that was it. Their one-night stand was done and dusted. He had lost count of how many such encounters he'd had over the years but never before had he wanted to change the rules. He had seen Sylvie as a challenge. The thrill of winning her over was supposed to feel like a victory but instead he felt a troubling sense of disappointment. A disturbing sense of wishing he hadn't agreed to just one night.

But a fling with a colleague, especially one who was acting for his client's estranged wife in a messy divorce created a dilemma for Jack. He preferred to keep his work and private life separate but Sylvie Rathbone had bewitched him into breaking his own rules. Making love with her was so damn satisfying and not just because he had seen her as a challenge. The sensuality of her touch, her soft responsive mouth, the smooth glide of her hands and her whimpering cries of pleasure kept replaying in his mind. Something about their union had touched him in a way he hadn't been touched before.

Sex for him was a physical thing, a body-based sensation that didn't intersect with his emotions. He didn't consider himself a particularly emotional person. He had been once but that was so long ago he could barely believe he was the same person as that small child who had received the news of his parents' death with such stoicism, when beneath the surface despair and dread and a deep aching sense of loss threatened to overwhelm him. But he had two younger brothers to care for and a grieving grandmother who needed him to be strong. So, that's what he had done.

He had become strong. But in doing so he'd had to deny what he was feeling in order to help and support those he loved. He had taught himself not to feel as a child and then a teenager. Every sexual encounter he had was a physical experience, not an emotional one. He had friendships, sure, people he cared about, but he never let things get too serious. He wanted his life free of complications. He veered away from long-term commitment because he didn't have the emotional software.

Jack wandered into his bedroom where only half an hour or so ago he and Sylvie had made passionate love. He looked at the rumpled bedcover and a hot shiver raced through his blood as he pictured her naked body entwined with his. How could he have thought one night with Sylvie Rathbone was going to be enough? And why wasn't it enough when normally he walked away from a sexual encounter without a qualm?

He wanted more and he sensed Sylvie did too, even

if she'd made it clear she was a career woman who had a busy legal practice to run. And why shouldn't they engage in a quick fling if it was what they both wanted? They could keep it private, especially since they were neighbours and they were unlikely to be outed by the intrusive press. As much as he wanted to go to her place right now and ask for more than just this night together, he decided to wait until the following evening.

He was so turned on at the thought, he could hardly wait.

When Sylvie arrived at work the following morning, Mariah peered at her suspiciously. 'Hey, what's happened?' she asked.

Sylvie smoothed down her skirt and straightened her designer jacket. 'What do you mean?'

'You look different.'

'How?'

'Your eyes are sparkling and you have beard rash.'

Sylvie put her hand up to her chin, frowning as she remembered the red circle of skin she had tried to cover with makeup but had clearly failed to do so adequately. 'It's a reaction to a skin cream.'

Mariah gave her a probing you-can't-fool-me look. 'If you ask me, I'd say you've broken your celibacy run. And clearly it was a huge success. Who was it? Anyone we know?'

Sylvie could feel a faint blush staining her cheeks. 'It was just a one-night thing.'

'Tell me more.' Mariah's eyes lit up like candles.

Sylvie turned to the coffee machine. 'There's nothing to tell. We agreed it was a one-off thing.'

Natasha came in at that point holding a stack of printed cards in her hand. Her gait had changed as her pregnancy had progressed and she was lumbering even slower than usual even though she still had a month to go before her due date. 'I finally got around to printing the baby shower cards. Here, this is one for you. I hope you can make it.'

Sylvie took the card from her and looked at the cute design with unicorns and rainbows and balloons and fairies and elves. 'I'd love to come. I've never been to a baby shower before.' She put the card in her briefcase and added, 'Or been a bridesmaid.'

'We would have asked you to be ours but my sister and cousin would've made such a fuss if they weren't asked,' Natasha said. 'Anyway, I thought you weren't keen on weddings.'

Sylvie gave them both a wry smile. 'Not every marriage is doomed to failure. Look at you two for example.'

Natasha and Mariah squeezed each other's hands. 'Yes, well, we're lucky we live in a time when our love is accepted and we *can* get married,' Mariah said.

'Did I tell you my mum is seeing someone?' Sylvie said.

Her colleagues both gaped at her. 'Seriously?' Natasha said. 'Have you met him or her?'

'He's a retired vet apparently. A lonely widower who was happily married until his wife died five years ago. Mum's going to introduce me to him soon.'

'How do you feel about that?' Mariah asked.

Sylvie cradled her mug in both of her hands. 'I'm cautiously optimistic, but she's been on her own for so long and I didn't think she would ever get over my father's rejection, so if this works out, it will give me a break from worrying about her all the time.'

Sylvie took a refreshing sip of coffee, glanced at the clock on the wall, and then put her cup down and picked up her briefcase. 'I'd better get moving. I have clients this morning and a court hearing this afternoon.'

'How are the Winterses' divorce proceedings going?'

'I haven't heard from Edwina in three days, which is a record. I've probably jinxed it now by talking about it.'

Sylvie walked up the corridor to her office a short time later to where her secretary was seated, her hand over the phone's mouthpiece. 'Sylvie, Edwina wants to see you tomorrow at 10:00 a.m. I can squeeze her in between Jeanne Blake and Zelda Poulous.'

Yep. She had jinxed it. 'Okay.'

Jack was finding it hard to concentrate, which was highly unusual for him. Normally he had laser focus when it came to work, but his thoughts kept circling back to Sylvie and what they had experienced together the night before. But then Hugo Winters arrived for a meeting and he had to put last night to one side while he listened to his client's ranting.

'I tell you, Jack, Edwina isn't fit to have full custody

of the children. I called on them yesterday and she was in bed with a hangover.'

Jack frowned. 'Are you sure it wasn't something else? A virus?'

Hugo leaned back in his chair with a heavy sigh. 'She's had a drinking problem ever since we were married. I didn't realise at first. Who doesn't love a drink or two at night? But then, I found hidden bottles of gin and vodka. She doesn't do it all the time, sometimes it's weeks, even months before she has a drink. I swear she hasn't been drunk in ages. I wasn't going to mention it before because I thought she was sober. I was more concerned about her lack of boundaries with the kids but she must've gone on a bender yesterday, so now I have this to worry about as well.'

'It's a serious allegation to make against someone. Do you have any witnesses, other than the children?'

Hugo looked defeated rather than his usual angry self. He shook his head. 'As I said, it's been literally years, two or three at least, since she's been drunk. She went to some meetings and seemed to have it under control.'

'What do you think triggered this bender?'

Hugo looked a little sheepish. 'Of course, the divorce is hard on both of us. But our daughter, Mimi, is a handful. She's a very emotional type, a bit like her mother. I think she needs toughening up. You can't go through life hiding under the bedcovers just because someone said something nasty to you. Edwina is way too soft on her. She lets her stay home if she doesn't feel up to going to school. I'm paying big money for the kids' education, and I want them both to attend regularly.'

'How's your son handling the divorce proceedings?'

Hugo shrugged. 'He's fine. He keeps to himself pretty much. He's at that age when you only get a grunt for an answer.'

'Do you spend any time with them both? Individually or one-on-one?' Jack asked, trying to get a picture of what sort of involvement Hugo had with his children.

'I'm too busy paying for everything,' Hugo said in a defensive tone. 'All this gentle parenting crap is ruining a whole generation of young people. They'll not be able to cope with a single setback in life. Edwina is too permissive. When I put my foot down over an issue, she undoes it all by letting the kids do what they want as soon as I turn my back.'

'What was your relationship like with your father?' It wasn't a question Jack usually asked a client, but in this case, he thought it might be important. Family patterns could be passed from generation to generation and if those patterns weren't positive, great damage could be done.

Hugo shifted in his chair, his eyes avoiding Jack's. 'It was all right, I guess. Didn't do me much harm, eh? I'm a successful businessman and live a very comfortable—'

'A successful businessman who is currently going through an acrimonious divorce,' Jack pointed out. The cynic in him wanted to know if Hugo was living such a comfortable life, why then was there no sign of great wealth in the financial documents Jack had been given by Hugo? They were still waiting to hear back from the independent forensic accountant, but Jack's guess was that all was not as it seemed and he wanted all the facts in front of him.

'Yes, well, that's Edwina's fault. I don't want to be married to a drunk. I don't want my kids to be neglected by her when she's off her head with booze.'

Jack flicked his pen between his thumb and index finger as he listened to Hugo describe how he often came home to a house of chaos and how hard it was for Hugo to run a business with his worries about the children's safety. They were genuine concerns if indeed what Hugo told him about Edwina was true. But in his experience in family law, there were always three sides to the story—his side, her side and the truth.

Jack was in search of the truth and wouldn't stop until he uncovered it.

Sylvie was sitting within a few feet of Shadow, who was eating the food she had put out as soon as she got home from work. The little cat was growing in confidence and size. She was no longer skinny with a lacklustre coat but filling out and her fur looked shiny and healthy. 'Here, Shadow—' Sylvie slowly held out her hand with a cat treat on the middle of her palm '—would you like this?'

The cat lifted her head from the bowl she was eating from, but this time, didn't dash away out of sight. She licked her mouth and twitched her long white whiskers and then stepped cautiously towards Sylvie's outstretched hand. 'Attagirl. I won't hurt you. You're safe with me,' Sylvie coaxed her with a soft voice.

The cat stopped within touching distance but Sylvie didn't rush things. She kept still, holding her hand out with the treat so Shadow could smell it. Shadow's green eyes stared at Sylvie unblinkingly, her body crouched low to the ground as if ready to run if she needed to.

'Here, I'll put it on this rock for you.' Sylvie carefully put the tiny fish-shaped treat on one of the garden rocks and then stayed still and quiet to see if the little cat would take it while she was there. The smell of the treat must have appealed to Shadow, for she crept closer, her eyes on Sylvie the whole time. But then there was the sound of Jack's bifold doors opening next door and Shadow darted off, leaving the treat behind.

Sylvie swore under her breath and crawled out from under the bushes and glared at Jack, who was now at the fence. 'Your timing is terrible,' she said.

'It seemed to be spot on last night.' His sardonic smile sent a wave of incendiary heat through her body.

She decided to ignore his comment because, apart from work, she had done nothing but think about their lovemaking last night. Her body recalled every kiss, every stroke of his hands and lips and tongue and the intimate coupling that made her flesh sing for hours afterwards. 'I was getting so close to her but you frightened her off.'

'Let's hope I don't do the same to you.' He vaulted over the fence like a gymnast and came over to where she was standing. 'I was hoping to see you tonight.'

'Oh?' Sylvie kept her tone indifferent even though every cell in her body was hanging on his next words.

'I saw Hugo Winters today.'

'And?'

'And I'd like to talk to you about what he told me. Your place or mine?'

Sylvie deliberated for a beat or two. 'My place.'

She led the way inside her kitchen-living area that was so similar to Jack's new extension, although Jack's appliances were top of the range and probably cost four times what hers had. 'Tea? Coffee? Wine? Spirits?' she asked.

'Whatever you're having.'

'I was having an herbal tea—camomile.'

Jack screwed up his face. 'I'm not a fan. I'll just have a glass of water.'

'You sure you don't want something stronger?'

'I need to keep a clear head.'

'Because?'

His eyes drifted to her mouth and her stomach did a jerky somersault. 'Because this is a business visit, not a personal one.'

'Well, of course it would be because we agreed on one night and one night only,' Sylvie said in a matter-of-fact tone, reaching for a tall glass and filling it from the water dispenser tap at her sink. She turned and handed it to him with a blank expression. His expression was etched in a frown as if her statement about their encounter last night annoyed him.

Jack took the glass from her but the brush of his fingers against hers seemed to send an erotic message from his body to hers. A tingle went from her fingers to her shoulder and beyond, making her recall his electrifying touch last night on her most intimate flesh. Yes, indeed, his timing had been spot on last night. No one had ever been able to get her to orgasm so spectacularly with just a flicker of his tongue.

'As I said, I met with Hugo Winters today,' Jack said.

'And?'

'Has Edwina ever mentioned she has a drinking problem?'

Sylvie frowned. 'No.'

Jack blew out a short breath. 'My client said he found her in a drunken stupor yesterday. He informed me she's had drinking issues for most of their married life but apparently got it under control from time to time. I got the impression this was the first time in a while but with two children to take care off, it's disturbing if this is going to continue. I will have no choice but to argue for him to receive full custody. The children's welfare and safety depend on her being a fit and capable parent. A history of getting blackout drunk is not going to help her case.'

Sylvie stared at him as his words hit her like flying stones. She would dodge one, only to be hit with another. How could this be true of her client? Her meek and shy and lacking-in-confidence client who loved her children so much she would do anything for them.

But then a doubt trickled like a muddy stain through her brain. What if she had got it wrong about Edwina Winters? What if Edwina was a closet drinker? Motherhood was tough. Sylvie had seen her own mother struggle with the responsibilities of providing for her under difficult circumstances. Her mother hadn't resorted to alcohol but there was a lot about Edwina that reminded her of her own mother. The victim status she clung to, the sense that she had done nothing to deserve what had happened to her, when Sylvie knew from years of family law work that relationship breakdowns were rarely one person's fault.

But pride wouldn't allow Sylvie to accept Jack's version of her client. She arched her brows at him, her arms folded against her chest. 'And you believed that fairy story word for word?'

'Come on, Sylvie.' Jack blew out a harsh breath of frustration. 'I know Hugo isn't father of the year or anything but what if those kids are driven to school by their mother the morning after a bender? She will still be over the legal limit, which will put those kids' lives in danger, not to mention other people on the road or indeed pedestrians.'

Sylvie brushed past him and paced the living room floor, trying to rein in her fury. She hated being blindsided by information she should have discovered herself. But she still wasn't one hundred percent convinced this was true. She turned and faced Jack again. 'I want evidence and not hearsay from a vindictive bully of a husband who wants out of his marriage. I'd also like a closer look at the financial statements—all of them, once the forensic accountant gets back to us.'

Jack scraped a hand through his thick hair, one strand falling forward over his right eye. 'I've been involved in cases where even the best forensic accountants haven't been able to track a client's money. Offshore banking, trust funds in other names—you'd be surprised at the lengths some people will go to, to avoid paying maintenance.'

'I'm not one bit surprised,' Sylvie retorted. 'Hugo Winters is one of many men I've come across who punish their ex-wives with poverty.'

The air crackled with a palpable tension that suddenly had nothing to do with the topic at hand. Sylvie wasn't sure at what point it changed but the atmosphere took on a new tension. Jack's eyes were locked on hers, hers were locked on his. She took a shaky breath to get control, to steady herself, to regulate her emotions. But the one thing she couldn't get control of was her desire for him. She could feel it building in her body—the uptick of her blood, the thickening of her female flesh, the dewy heat between her thighs.

Jack looked at her mouth at the same time she looked at his. She wasn't sure who moved first or if they both moved at the same moment, but suddenly his arms were around her and his mouth was on hers and she was whimpering with encouragement and delight. It was an angry kiss at first, a kiss that spoke of tensions between them that were not resolved and would not be for some time.

But then his kiss changed, softened, deepened, his tongue meeting hers and mating in a dance as old as time itself. It was sensual, passionate and yet tender at the same time. A beguiling kiss between two people who had agreed on one night only but their kiss and their response to each other's touch told otherwise. Never had Sylvie wanted a man more than Jack Wilde.

It infuriated her that it was him who had set her on fire. Who had unlocked her sensuality and caused her to crave him like a potent drug. She didn't like that he had such power over her. She thought she could play the same game he did—the casual approach to sex. The one-nighter. The fling without strings. But making love with him once had awakened a fierce hunger inside her that only he could assuage. She wanted him with a ferocious longing, and she hated herself for it.

Would she turn into her mother? Craving a man who had no intention of being faithful or settling down? Did she even want to settle down? The questions were flying around her head even as his tongue was doing wicked things to the skin of her neck—licking, stroking, tearing down her willpower like it was tissue paper and not steel.

'I want you so bad,' Jack groaned against her lips, his aroused body flush against her, leaving her in no doubt of what he wanted. It was what she wanted too, and she toyed with denying it…for about a nanosecond. How could she deny this rush of feeling? This erotic primal urge that she already knew could be stupendous. It would be different if she hadn't already experienced his magical lovemaking, easier to brush off what she didn't know existed.

But she did know. She knew every tingling moment of being in his arms and she wanted him again. They could keep it casual—she would insist on it. She couldn't allow herself to turn into a version of her mother, falling for a man who could never love her completely, exclusively.

Sylvie had heard the gossip years ago about Jack sleeping with a married woman. It went against all her principles and yet, she hadn't heard Jack's side of the story. And now that she understood, fully understood, the intense drives and urges and explosive chemistry that two people could ignite in each other, she felt less inclined to judge.

Lust was something that had slammed into her defences, collapsing them like a house of cards in its hurricane force. It was unstoppable, irresistible and she wanted to feel his body moving inside hers again until she shattered into a thousand pieces.

Sylvie wrapped her arms around his neck, her slight body pressed tightly against him as his arms held her like he never wanted to let her go. 'I want you too,' she whispered against his lips, teasing them into another electrifying kiss. A few breathless moments later, Jack eased away, looking down at her with eyes gleaming darkly as wet paint.

'What about our one-night rule?'

'We can make the rules as we go along. I'm not going to ask you to go on bended knee and whip out a flashy diamond. I don't want that. This is all I want.' And she put her mouth back on his and was swept away on a tide of unstoppable passion.

CHAPTER EIGHT

JACK WONDERED IF he would ever tire of kissing Sylvie's soft and responsive mouth. Her lips clung to his, her tongue dancing with his in a dance that sent blood thumping to his groin with incendiary heat. He loved the vanilla milkshake taste of her mouth, the way her petite body pressed so keenly against his, as if she wanted to melt into him completely.

But it wasn't just the physical closeness that stirred him so deeply. He felt a deep sense of camaraderie with her. Was it because they were both divorce lawyers and cynical about love? Jack had taught himself to ignore the human need to love. To ignore the need to be connected in a deep and lasting way with another person. The sort of love that made your bones ache to be near the other person, to touch them, to hold them, to commit to them. The sort of love that filled your chest and made it hard to take a breath without feeling its gentle tug. The sort of love that could be obliterated in a few seconds, love that could be snatched away, extinguished when you needed it most, leaving you empty, lost, abandoned, vulnerable and that most wretched feeling of all—loneliness.

Jack wasn't the sort of man on a lifelong quest to find a soulmate. He wasn't even convinced such a thing existed. Humans were flawed and so were their relationships, even the best ones. Since his parents' death, he had never pictured himself growing old with someone, raising a family and doing all the things long-term couples do. He was too aware of how it all could be taken away in the blink of an eye. Like his parents had been taken from him. One minute he was part of a happy family, the next he was an orphan along with his brothers. His ability to love deeply forever shattered like the fuselage of his parents' plane.

His career was his entire focus. He had always loved the challenge of winning a case for a client. The fight for justice was something that motivated him to get out of bed each morning. With the eye-watering wealth he came from, he could have easily taken over his grandfather's business interests, but studying law had appealed to him from a young age, plus it maintained his independence from his controlling and difficult grandfather. His career was everything he needed it to be—intense, thrilling, fulfilling, demanding and financially rewarding. His background in law had helped him expand his financial interests into stocks and shares and property investment, similar to his brother Jago.

He and his brothers might not be as close as three orphaned brothers ought to be, but they had each fought to be independent of their grandfather rather than become trust fund kids, which they easily could have done given the Wilde family wealth.

But now, with his mouth on Sylvie's and her arms

wrapped around his neck, Jack's desire to be a playboy was losing its shine and it scared him. It freaked him out to think he was starting to feel things he didn't want to feel for someone who had no intention of feeling the same for him.

In a weird reversal, it was Sylvie who had insisted on a one-night stand and while he had accepted it at the time, he couldn't help feeling uneasy about the control taken so neatly out of his hands. He was the one who defined how long a fling would last…not that any of his flings lasted long. He lost interest once the chase was over but with Sylvie, he was ambushed by feelings he had never expected to feel. The need for more time with her, more of her touch and taste, more of her spine-tingling response to him that made him feel more of a man than he had ever felt before. Was it just simple physical chemistry? An electric chemistry that drew them together in spite of their differences about their clients?

Sylvie eased her mouth away and looked up at him with eyes luminous with desire. The same desire he was trying to control in his body. A pounding drive to get naked and down to business, to release the build-up of sexual tension that was at an unbearable level because of one passionate kiss. 'Are you game to risk another night with me?' There was a spark of challenge in her brown eyes.

'I'm game,' Jack said, moving his mouth down the side of her neck to breathe in her flowery scent. He teased her earlobe with his tongue and she shivered and turned her head so her mouth could reach his.

She put her hands on either side of his face, her lips pressing down on his in a hot kiss that promised earth-shattering passion.

Jack took control of the kiss, deepening it with a gliding movement of his tongue that made her breathe a soft murmur of delight. Her tongue danced with his and his blood pounded so hard all he could think of was getting her beneath him.

This time it was Sylvie who led him to her bedroom but as for him getting her beneath him, she clearly had other ideas. She took charge by pushing him down on her bed with a surprisingly firm hand on his chest, then came down overtop of him to straddle him.

Jack reached up and released her chestnut hair and it tumbled in fragrant waves over her neck and shoulders. He ran his fingers through the silky strands and watched as the pleasure of his touch played out on her exquisite features. Even though they were both still dressed, he could feel the pressure of her body against his arousal and he had to fight to maintain control. Desire roared through him like the backdraft of a wildfire. Every cell in his body throbbed to possess her, to slide into her hot velvety warmth and take them both to paradise.

But Sylvie wasn't finished teasing him. She feathered tiny kisses all over his face, then moved down to unbutton his shirt, planting more kisses over his chest, then taking each of his flat nipples in her teeth in a kitten nip that sent sparks shooting down his spine. She went lower with her tongue, licking, stroking, teasing until she came to his belly button. She dipped her tongue into the tight whorl of his flesh, then went lower still, unzipping his trousers and peeling down his underwear.

Jack sucked in a breath, his blood pounding like a tribal drum, a primal urge to have her take him in her mouth sending his pulse rate soaring. He made a sound that was largely unintelligible because his voice box was blocked by the erotic sight of her pulling her hair over one shoulder and then going down on him.

By some miracle he managed to get a condom into her hands and she gave him a sultry look and unpeeled it, then applied it to him slowly, torturously slowly. He was gritting his teeth, his jaw, thinking of everything he could to take his mind off the need to let go. Sylvie was in control of him, not him of her and it was thrilling, exciting, mind-blowing. *Bliss...*

Jack needed a minute or two to recover and watched as she undressed in front of him with a complete lack of modesty. It thrilled him to see her so confident in herself. It turned him on all over again.

'Come here,' he commanded.

'I'm coming.'

'Damn straight you are as long as I've got anything to do with it,' Jack said, the double entendre deliberate.

Sylvie shook her hair back and came over to the bed, close enough for him to capture her hand and pull her down to join him. This time, he made sure she was underneath him. He worshipped her body from top to toe and teased her flesh until she was begging him to finish her off. He tasted her essence but didn't let her come. He waited until he drove inside her tight wet warmth and thrusted vigorously, groaning along with her cries of encouragement until they both flew into oblivion…

Sometime later, Sylvie left Jack sleeping and carefully eased herself out of his hold, reached for her wrap and slipped it on to cover her nakedness. Her body was still tingling from the sensations he had made her feel. She went out to her kitchen to get a glass of water. Who knew making love could be so energetic, so physically satisfying, much more satisfying than her hot yoga sessions. She looked out at the back garden, checking to see if Shadow had eaten the rest of the food. She had placed the dish a little closer to her back door each day. Sylvie was relieved to see the dish was empty, although there was no sign of the little cat.

Sylvie replayed her lovemaking session with Jack, shivering as she recalled his expert touch. No one had ever made her feel what he made her feel, which meant she would have to be careful to end things before she got too addicted to his touch.

She was proud of herself for taking charge of their sexual encounters. She refused to be yet another simpering woman who begged him to extend their time together. So far, she was in control of her feelings. It was physical between them, a mutual itch they were scratching, but it had no future. Not just because neither of them were looking to settle down, but also because they were on opposing sides of a difficult divorce case, one Sylvie was determined to win for her client.

But the troubling news Jack had delivered before

they got distracted by their lust for each other was gnawing away at her. What if she had got Edwina Winters wrong? What if Edwina played the victim so convincingly, Sylvie hadn't picked up on other issues that could have a powerful impact on the custody battle? She hated being blindsided and had always prided herself on being a good judge of character. She could usually pick a fraud a mile off, but what if Edwina had hidden the ugly truth from her about her issues around alcohol?

She heard a sound behind her and turned to see Jack coming towards her, wearing his clothes now, although his shirt was unbuttoned, revealing his tanned and muscular chest.

He smiled one of his bone-melting dimpled smiles and came over to wrap his arms around her and hold her close. 'I was wondering where you got to.' His deep voice was like a caress down the length of her spine.

Sylvie eased back to look up at him. 'I'm sorry I was so defensive about what you told me about Edwina Winters.'

'I think we very satisfactorily resolved our differences, hmm?' He bent down to nibble gently at her earlobe, sending her senses into free fall.

'Yes, well, it was a good distraction, but I have to see her to hear her side of the story.' Sylvie linked her arms around his trim waist, struggling to keep her emotions in check. It felt so wonderful to be held by him. His height could easily have been intimidating—it once was—but now she felt safe in his gentle and protective hold. She was familiar with every inch of his skin, craved the feel of it against her own. He was an exciting lover, the most exciting and satisfying lover she had ever had.

Jack cupped her face in his hands and planted a brief firm kiss on her lips, then straightened, his expression set in more serious lines. 'I want to see you again.' There was an intractable edge to his tone.

Sylvie released an uneven breath. 'Jack…it's too dangerous. What if someone sees us?'

A glint came into his eyes. 'I think it's the danger element that makes it all the more enjoyable. Who's going to see us? We can keep it under wraps here or at my place.'

'I don't know…' She chewed her lip for a moment, torn between the temptation of having more time with him but the dreaded fear of exposure. Putting herself in a compromising position was a deep concern. She didn't want to be so distracted by Jack that she didn't represent her client to the best of her ability. He was not only distracting, but also her opponent in a court of law. Could she successfully compartmentalise her personal life from her professional?

The stakes for her were much higher than for Jack. Everyone already knew he was a playboy but she had always kept her private life private. She had always made sure her work came first. No exceptions. But Jack had made her world tilt on its axis and she didn't know how to get her equilibrium back, and that was scary. Scary and deeply troubling.

'I have an even better idea,' Jack said, tilting up her

chin to mesh her gaze with his gleaming one. 'Let's go to Paris for the weekend. We can fly by private jet and—'

'Private jet?' Sylvie's eyes goggled like a goldfish's.

He shrugged off her comment. 'I'm a Wilde brother. We fly by private jet when we want to. It's more convenient and—'

'And completely self-indulgent and shrieks of outrageous privilege.'

'All true but I didn't choose my heritage any more than you chose yours.'

Sylvie eased out of his hold and folded her arms across her middle. She couldn't think clearly when he had his hands on her. The electrical charge of his touch scrambled her operating system like a hacked computer. She'd been hacked by Jack and so far, did not have the software to deal with it. 'I have a baby shower this weekend. If I accept your offer, it will have to be the weekend after that.'

'Okay, that's fine. I have to check on my grandparents and catch up with Jonas anyway. He hasn't confirmed it but he was hoping to fly home to Wildewood this weekend.'

'You must be excited to see him after so long.'

'Yes and no. I want to wring his neck for not responding to my texts or emails for eight months. Jago's angry he hasn't been able to get married, and my grandmother could have died after a fall a few weeks back but we had no way of contacting Jonas other than leaving yet another voice message. And I had the unseemly task of trying to convince his girlfriend that he was no longer interested. I'm sure she thought I was lying the whole time.' He scraped his hair back with his hand and then flashed one of his easy-going smiles, no doubt to lighten the atmosphere that had become so serious. 'Sorry, I'm probably boring you with my wacko family stuff.'

'On the contrary, I find it rather fascinating,' Sylvie said. 'Mine is so very different.'

He came over to her and, holding her face with both hands, planted a swift but still sensual kiss to her lips. 'You'll have to tell me all about it in Paris.'

He was at the door, preparing to leave before she could think of a response. 'I haven't said I'm going yet.'

He winked at her, his smile annoyingly self-assured. 'You will.' And then he was gone.

CHAPTER NINE

As soon as Sylvie opened the door of conference room three the following morning, Edwina jumped out of her seat, face flushed and her bobbed hair in disarray. 'I'm so sorry to ask for this last-minute appointment, but you won't believe the lengths Hugo is going to this time to ruin my chances of custody.'

'I'm sorry to hear that,' Sylvie said. 'Sit down and tell me what's been going on.'

Edwina sat down, her hands twisted together in her lap, her agitation distressing to witness.

'He's spreading rumours that I'm drinking again. I swear I gave it up when I got pregnant. I've been sober for years. I know I had a problem once but I don't drink now. But he came to see the kids the other night and I had a migraine and had taken one of my painkillers that makes me sleepy. He accused me of being hungover and called me some horrible names and then…' she pulled out a tissue and dabbed at her streaming eyes '…after he left, I found Mimi cutting herself in her bedroom.'

She burst into tears as she stumbled on. 'She only made little cuts on her arms, not big enough to take her to hospital, but still… I have to get out of this marriage, but how do I do it without damaging the kids any further? I can't bear the thought of Hugo looking after them. He never did much for them while we were together, so how likely is it he's going to do everything for them once he has them?'

'Oh, Edwina, I'm so sorry for what you and the kids are going through,' Sylvie said, pushing a box of tissues across the table so her client could reach them.

Edwina rummaged in her purse and showed Sylvie a prescription medication. 'These are the pills I take when I have a migraine. They can make me very groggy and out of it for a while.'

Sylvie glanced at the label and noted the listed side effects. 'I'm glad you came in and told me.'

'So…you believe me?' The watery hope in Edwina's eyes was heart-wrenching to see.

'Of course I do. Now, take yourself home and try and support the kids, especially Mimi, through this difficult time.' She opened the folder she'd brought with her and took out a sheet with a list of recommended psychologists she always kept nearby and handed it to her client. 'I know you already have a lot on your plate but here are the contact details of some supportive psychologists who can help you with Mimi.'

Edwina took the sheet and folded it into a square and slipped it into her purse. 'I don't know how to thank you. You've been so kind and supportive to me.'

Sylvie rose from her chair. 'Take care of yourself, Edwina.'

'I'm trying to.' Edwina gave a strained smile and stood. 'Thanks again.'

Once Edwina left, Sylvie sank back into her chair and let out a gusty sigh. She only hoped her client never found out she was sleeping with her husband's lawyer. 'Oh God.' She put her head in her hands and gave a mental scream of frustration. 'What have I got myself into?'

Jack got home that evening and went outside to see if Sylvie's cat had been for a visit. The food he had put out was gone, so either it was the cat or the rat that was feasting on the best cat food money could buy. He looked across at Sylvie's house but there was no sign she was home yet. The dip in his mood surprised him. He wasn't the sort of guy to catch feelings for women he dated, but he genuinely had been looking forward to seeing Sylvie after work.

He turned to go back inside his house when he saw Sylvie enter her kitchen-living space that was so like his own. She tossed her bag on the sofa and then turned and saw him looking at her. Her expression soured and she stomped out her back door and over to the fence that divided their properties.

'I want a word with you,' she said through tight lips.

'I want much more than that with you,' Jack said with a grin. 'Has anyone told you how cute you look when you're pretending to be angry?'

'Pretending?' She drew herself up to her full height. 'I'm not angry—I'm furious.'

'What about?'

'Your client.'

'Which one?'

'You know damn well which one.' Her eyes were spitting sparks of fire.

Jack hopped over the fence and came and stood in front of her. 'Look, I get that he's not a great guy but if his wife is an alcoholic then—'

'It's all lies,' Sylvie said. 'Edwina was taking painkillers for a migraine when he turned up unannounced. What your client witnessed was the side effects of pain meds, not a hangover.'

Jack hadn't taken a painkiller in his life, but his younger brother Jonas had suffered from severe headaches a few months before he went on his mission abroad. Jack had witnessed the powerful effect of the meds on his brother and could see how easily—or conveniently in Hugo Winters's case—the side effects could be mistaken for being drunk. Jack thought Sylvie had been hoodwinked by her client but now he realised with an unsettled feeling in his gut that he had been the one to be fooled by Hugo Winters. Was he so distracted by Sylvie he wasn't on top of his game?

He didn't have to like his clients but he had to give them his all. It gave him an uneasy feeling to be so consumed by his fling with Sylvie that he was missing clues he normally wouldn't miss. It more or less confirmed his stance on the wisdom of not mixing business with pleasure, but he didn't want their fling to end just yet. He craved her company and touch too much.

Jack scraped a hand through his hair. 'Okay, so I'll have another chat with my client. There are always three sides to the story you know—his side, her side and the truth.'

Sylvie blew out a breath of frustration. 'It's their daughter I'm worried about. After Hugo left, Edwina found Mimi cutting herself in her bedroom.'

Jack frowned. 'How badly?'

'Just light scratches but these things can escalate. I've given my client a list of psychologists to see but it may be weeks or even months before she gets an appointment.'

Jack reached out and brushed a stray strand of hair back from Sylvie's face and gently tucked it behind her ear. She didn't flinch or back away but stood and seemed to relax under his touch. 'You really go all in for your clients.'

'Don't you?'

He gave a rueful grimace. 'Yes, but not with the sensitivity and care you do. I just take their money and fight like hell for them.'

Sylvie's eyes glittered. 'You can't win this one, Jack. It will destroy those kids, not to mention my client.'

Jack rolled a shutter down on his emotions. 'Let's not talk about work. Have you seen Shadow today?'

'No, but the food is gone and I'm luring her closer to the house each time I feed her.'

'Clever tactic. I might try that.'

Sylvie put her head to one side. 'Are you trying to steal my cat?'

Jack put his arms around her and drew her close. 'No, but right now I'd like to steal a kiss if that's okay with you.'

A sparkling light came into her eyes. 'Steal away.'

And so, he did.

* * *

Natasha and Mariah's baby shower was held at their townhouse in Croydon. Sylvie handed around food and drinks to help out as there were a lot of guests—both sets of very excited grandparents-to-be, sisters, cousins, friends, associates and neighbours. It was a gender reveal party as well and it was hard not to get caught up in the excitement, especially as Natasha and Mariah were not only her close friends but also partners in her law firm.

'It's a boy!' Natasha's mother cried out for joy. There were whoops and cheers all round and while Sylvie joined in, a part of her began to question her stance against settling down and having children. It was as if the foundation on which she had built her life was feeling a little unsteady. Was her relationship with Jack to blame? Was the exquisite sex they had together making her question everything she had thought she wanted?

Of course it was crazy to think Jack might fall in love with her and want to marry her and have children. It was even crazier to think she was falling in love with him…and yet…his touch evoked such sensations in her body. And not just in her body but in her mind. She enjoyed his easy-going company. He didn't take life as seriously as her, which counterbalanced her tendency to be pessimistic.

'Here,' Natasha said, handing her a glass of champagne. 'You've been so busy serving everyone else I haven't seen you relax for a minute.'

'Thanks.' Sylvie took the champagne and took a tiny sip. 'Mmm, lovely. It's a great baby shower.'

'I thought you might find it boring since you're not interested in babies.'

'I love babies and kids,' Sylvie said. 'I just haven't thought I'd ever want them.' Natasha perched on the edge of the sofa next to Sylvie, absently stroking the huge mound of her abdomen. 'Are you saying you've changed your mind?'

Sylvie gave a small smile. 'I'm not sure what I want. I used to be so black and white about everything but lately I've been extending my horizons a bit.'

'Has it got anything to do with Jack Wilde?'

Sylvie frowned. 'Why would it have anything to do with him?'

'Clare from Accounts saw you two dancing at the fundraiser. She said he took you out on the balcony and you stayed out there for ages.'

'We were discussing the Winterses' divorce.'

Natasha gave her a you-can't-fool-me look.

Sylvie let out a breath. 'He's hard to avoid and besides, he's my neighbour.'

Natasha's eyes threatened to pop out of their sockets. 'Oh really? How convenient.'

Sylvie mock-glowered at her. 'It's damn inconvenient. Once our fling is over, I'll have a ringside seat to watch him work his way through hundreds of women, who, like me, couldn't resist him.'

'Oh, babe, you have got yourself into a mess, haven't you?'

Sylvie had buried her feelings, stashing them deep inside so she wouldn't be overwhelmed by them, but it was like trying to stop Ping-Pong balls floating in a bucket of water. 'I'll be fine. It's just sex. I'm surprised it's lasted this long.'

'How long?'

'Since the ball.'

Natasha squeezed Sylvie's shoulders in a supportive embrace. 'You're a strong woman. You'll get through this. You never know, it might actually turn out in the end.'

Sylvie stretched her lips into a strained smile. 'I doubt it but at least it's been one hell of an experience.'

Jack had been to Paris many times but never had been looking forward to a trip more than this one. He hadn't seen much of Sylvie as his grandfather came down with a stomach bug and Jack took a few days off work to visit. The irascible old man could be difficult at any time but particularly so when he was unwell. Jack knew his grandmother would appreciate a visit from him to distract her from the demands of Maxwell, who stubbornly refused to be 'fussed over' by a nurse.

Jonas had cancelled his trip home citing some hiccup in the project he had to see to but he'd assured Jack he would be home in a matter of weeks. Jack then had to placate Jago and Mollie about yet another delay to their wedding, but the date was now set and both Jack and Jago and Mollie had come to the decision it would go ahead with Jonas or without.

Jack packed a weekend bag and texted Sylvie to meet him at the airport. He saw her through the crowd of travellers—it was as if he had radar tuned into her frequency. He winked at her from a distance and her cautious smile reminded him of how cloak and dagger they had to be about their relationship.

Relationship? He baulked at the word like a horse shying at a jump. *Fling? Arrangement?* He couldn't think of a word that adequately described what their involvement was other than something they both enjoyed. For now. Sylvie had made it clear she wasn't interested in settling down, a claim he had been making about himself for his entire adult life. And yet, something about her setting the limits on their involvement made him feel a little edgy. He wasn't used to being the vulnerable one, the one who wanted more. But hey, did he want more? How much more? He wasn't the type of man to get emotionally invested in a relationship, especially a casual one.

But lately, he was finding it hard to think of his relationship with Sylvie as casual. Yes, they were having a fling and no doubt it would end soon because he always ended them before his lovers got any crazy ideas about commitment but… That annoying 'but' was triggering him more and more.

He liked Sylvie's company; he liked her feisty nature and her softer side she took great pains to hide. Her dedication to taming a wild cat for instance. Sylvie was driven like him and he admired her for it. Law was a tough career and could have a deleterious impact on your emotions if you didn't park them to one side, which, fortunately for him, he had been doing since he was seven.

This trip away to Paris would at least give him more time to enjoy Sylvie's company without the threat of exposure. It was convenient they lived next door to each other, which was entirely a coincidence, a pleasant one as it turned out. Jack bought the run-down property because it was a good location and he had the money to turn it into a dream home. But he hadn't factored in living next door to an ex-lover, which at some point, Sylvie would be. He didn't do long-term. He didn't do commitment. But then, Sylvie didn't want either of those things, so it was safe to extend their fling as long as they both wanted.

They went through security separately and it was only when they were on Jack's jet and finally alone that he leaned down to kiss her soft, irresistible mouth. 'Hello. Mmm, you smell gorgeous.' He breathed in the scent of flowers and fragrant summer evenings on her body, and hunger crawled through him to feel her skin naked against his.

Sylvie clipped her seat belt in place and gave him a cautious smile. 'I feel like I've entered a different world. I don't even fly business class even though I can afford to.'

'I've never flown any other way,' Jack said. 'Or at least not since my parents' death.'

'Weren't they flying on a smaller plane when they were killed?'

Jack grimaced. 'Yeah, I think it was my dad's way of standing up to my grandfather. He hired a smaller plane rather than take my grandfather's. He wanted more freedom but Maxwell was and still is a control freak.'

There was a moment of silence.

'Do you remember much about them?' Sylvie asked.

Jack gave a nostalgic smile. 'Dad was a fun guy to be around, that is when he was around, which wasn't much. Mum was beautiful and good to us but to be honest, she only had eyes for my dad. I didn't see it at the time, but looking back, my parents were always searching for excuses to get away together. I think they found the responsibility of parenting three young boys a bit boring. Gran raised us after they died but she was already doing that before they were killed.'

'She sounds like a lovely lady.'

'She is,' Jack said. 'I'd love you to meet her.'

'Is that a good idea?' Sylvie asked, sending him a sideways glance.

Jack suddenly realised the path he was heading down. Taking Sylvie to Wildewood to meet his grandparents was hardly the agenda of a hardened playboy and yet, he wanted his gran to meet Sylvie. He wanted to show Sylvie his childhood haunts and share with her some of his memories of his parents.

It was unusual for him to want any lover of his to cross the boundary line into his private life but Sylvie didn't have any plans to settle down. She didn't want the fairy tale. She just wanted him for sex. He should be pleased she ticked all the boxes for the perfect temporary lover but a niggling thought wormed its way through his brain…maybe, for the first time ever, he wanted more than a temporary fling.

He gave himself a mental slap hard enough to give himself a concussion. No way was he going to fall in love. He wasn't wired that way. Maybe if his parents hadn't died, he might have been the type of person who wanted marriage and kids, long-term companionship, and the richness and blessings of having someone as a witness to your life. He had friends who were happily married and he had older colleagues who had remained with their spouse for decades and been contented with their life together.

But it wasn't for him.

Jack had made that decision a long time ago.

Sylvie had been to Paris a couple of times, but staying in budget hotels was nothing to what it was like staying at a luxury hotel in the Latin Quarter, especially with Jack Wilde as her companion. Within moments of arriving, they were escorted to their penthouse suite where champagne and lush ripe strawberries and artfully assembled canapés were waiting to be consumed.

She tried not to show how impressed she was but it was yet another reminder of the two different worlds she had Jack had come from. He took this sort of luxury and privilege for granted. She had worked her butt off to rise above her poverty-stricken background, so every soft-as-a-cloud scatter cushion on the plush sofa, the knee-deep high-quality carpet, the artworks, the lighting, the crystal champagne flutes were things she saw as markers of how hard she had worked to enjoy such luxuries. She didn't think she would ever take such things for granted, no matter how much money she earned.

Jack shrugged off his jacket and tossed it over the back of the nearest sofa. 'I've booked dinner for us in a quaint restaurant a block or two from here. But we've plenty of time to freshen up.'

'Wonderful,' Sylvie said, going over to the window to look at the view below their suite. The Seine River was visible below; the beautiful Parisian architecture giving the scene an Old World atmosphere that was enchanting. 'Everything is wonderful.'

Jack came over to the window and put his hands on her shoulders and she leaned back into the hard frame of his body, her desire for him stirring in her blood. He turned her so she was facing him, his gaze meshing with hers in a spine-tingling lock. 'I'm going to take a shower. Do you want to join me?'

Sylvie's eyes sparkled impishly. 'You mean so we save water?' Her lips twitched as she tried not to smile. 'I'm all for looking after the planet.'

Jack pulled her even closer, his mouth coming down to within reach of hers. 'I want to make love to you so badly it's all I can think about.'

Sylvie wound her arms around his neck and stretched up on tiptoe. 'What's stopping you?'

'Nothing,' he said, and crushed her mouth beneath his.

CHAPTER TEN

An hour and a half later, Jack and Sylvie were dining in an exclusive restaurant a short walk from their hotel. Jack held up his glass towards hers. 'I propose a toast. Let's not talk about work but only about ourselves. I want to hear about your childhood. You've heard plenty about mine but I know virtually nothing about yours.'

Sylvie held her own glass up to clink against his, but her thoughts were in turmoil. She hated talking about her past life. She had moved so far away from her childhood circumstances it was like it had happened to a different person. In many ways, she *was* a different person. She had morphed into the person she needed to be to survive in the competitive field of law. 'O-kay,' she said. 'No talking about work.'

'What's your first memory?' Jack asked.

Sylvie screwed up her forehead, filtering through a host of unpleasant memories looking for one sanitised enough to share. 'We once went camping in the Lake District and it rained solidly the whole time. I was four. We never went camping again.'

Jack grimaced as if the thought of all that rain and sleeping in tents was anathema to him given his wealthy background. 'My first memory is when my mother brought home Jago after he was born. There's two years between each of us. I know you're not supposed to remember anything much before you're about three, but apparently I was excited to be having a brother and when I first saw him, he was all wizened up like an old man, and he did nothing but cry. I was bitterly disappointed. But maybe my parents told me how I reacted and it's not really a memory.' His expression became shadowed, and a dart hit Sylvie in the heart. Jack's earlier frown made her wonder if his normally lighthearted approach to life was to cover his deep sense of loss. His laugh was deep and melodious, and it was impossible not to want to hear it again and again and yet she wanted to hear his true feelings about his childhood too.

'What about when Jonas came along? Were you disappointed in him too?'

A ghost of worry floated through his gaze before he reset his expression into one of relaxed enjoyment at sharing childhood memories. 'Well, I was four by then and a bit more aware of how it would impact on me having not one but two younger brothers. Although Jonas was a quieter baby. He slept a lot and kept to himself, even as a toddler.'

'I would've loved a brother or sister,' Sylvie said, putting her wine glass down and flicking him a quick upwards glance. 'I think it would have made my life a little easier during my parents' divorce.'

'Tell me about how that was for you.'

'You sound like a relationships counsellor.'

Jack's eyes grew soft and caring. 'I was aiming more for a concerned friend.'

Sylvie arched her brows. 'Are we friends or just lovers?' She picked her wine glass up again and continued, 'I mean, once we end this, I can hardly see us exchanging pleasantries if we run into each other.' She took a sip of her wine before he answered.

'It doesn't have to be that way.'

Her look was still sceptical. 'Are you on speaking terms with your hundreds of ex-lovers?'

'Although I've lost count, I can assure you it's not in the hundreds.'

Sylvie shrugged as if it didn't bother her either way. 'Break-ups are hard the longer people stay together. My parents were married seemingly happily for ten years and then suddenly my father left. My mother was utterly devastated. She didn't see it coming. She was blindsided and heartbroken and it took her until very recently to get over it.'

'And you?'

'What about me?'

'Were you devastated?'

Sylvie moved her lips from side to side, not sure she wanted to reveal her feelings about that time. But then she thought of how devastated Jack and his brothers must have been after their parents were killed, so she decided to tell him. Death was much harder to deal with than divorce, although some would beg to differ.

'I didn't have the space to examine my feelings because my mother was so shattered. I had to be strong for her. I had to step up and take control because she was an emotional mess for months on end. Years actually.' She paused for a moment, and Jack reached across the table and took her free hand and gave it a gentle squeeze of comfort and support.

She lifted her gaze to his and continued with a scratchy voice, 'My father loved me until he didn't. Or maybe he never loved me or my mum. Maybe he wasn't capable of it. He certainly gave us a good impression of it at the time though. But then he disappeared from our lives and never fought to see me. He remarried and had another family, but I have no desire to see him or my step-siblings.'

'I don't blame you. What a jerk some men can be.'

Sylvie pulled her hand away from Jack's, suddenly feeling exposed and vulnerable in a way she wasn't used to feeling. She so rarely spoke of her background, even her friends and work colleagues knew only the basics, but with Jack she had felt comfortable to reveal more than she ever had before, which was weird because he wasn't exactly the stay-forever-in-a-relationship type of guy. What would he know of love and commitment and loyalty for life?

'Hey.' Jack's voice was soft but deep, calling for her to look at him.

Sylvie lifted her gaze back to his and her chest fluttered like a hummingbird was trapped in each of her heart valves. How could she resist him when he was so caring, so interested in her life's story?

'Has your father ever reached out to you?'

'No and I wouldn't see him if he did. He nearly destroyed my mother just so he could have his freedom. I can never forgive him for that.'

'Divorce brings out the worst in some people and the best in others,' Jack said. 'I think my grandmother would've divorced my grandfather if it hadn't been for my parents' death. She was trapped by looking after us. She made the most of it, of course, because that's the type of person she is—she always puts others before her own needs.'

'She sounds like an amazing grandmother.'

Jack gave a crooked smile. 'Yeah, she's one of the best, but don't tell her or she'll get a big head and be unbearable like my grandfather.'

'Like I said, when would I ever meet her?' Sylvie asked. 'It's not as if you're going to introduce me to your family.'

There was a pulsing silence.

Sylvie could see a host of micro expressions move over his face—the flicker of his gaze, the tightening of his jaw, the deep swallow that made his Adam's apple rise and fall. He opened his mouth as if he were going to say something but then he clamped it shut again. He picked up his wine glass and took a small sip, then placed the glass back on the table with a definitive thump.

'First hobby,' he said, changing the subject so abruptly Sylvie sat staring at him blankly for a beat or two.

'Erm… I used to press flowers. My mother showed me how to do it with baking paper and a thick book. I didn't have a proper flower press. I'd pick the blooms on my walk home from school. I think I did it because we didn't have a garden of our own.'

'And you longed for one?'

Sylvie met his searching gaze. 'I hated the complex we lived in. The police were there nearly every day for a domestic violence episode or a fight between rival drug gangs. It certainly wasn't an ideal place for a small child but my mother did her best to keep a roof over our heads.'

'Your mum sounds as wonderful as my gran.'

'I'd introduce you to her but then she'd think we were in love.'

Another beat or two of intense silence.

'Why would she think that?' His tone was mild but his gaze was suddenly intense.

'I've never introduced a partner to her before.'

A frown dug a trench between his eyes. 'How long have any of your relationships lasted?'

Sylvie gave him a pointed look. 'How long have any of yours lasted?'

Jack rubbed a hand over the light stubble on his jaw. 'None have lasted as long as you and I have.' His voice was deep and did strange fluttering things to the floor of her belly.

'Do you think we should end it after we leave Paris?' Sylvie asked in what she hoped was an indifferent, I-don't-care-either-way tone.

'No. We've managed to stay under the radar so far. And we're both having a good time, aren't we?' His eyes glinted at her meaningfully and a hot shiver rolled down her spine. He made sure she had a good time. She couldn't remember anyone making her feel as good as he did. And no, she didn't want it to end, but neither did she want to be caught in a compromising position given Jack was her client's husband's lawyer in one of the most acrimonious divorces of her legal career.

'I wouldn't have come with you if I wasn't having a good time, Jack,' Sylvie said in a soft voice.

Jack reached for one of her hands and cupped it in his. He stroked the back of it with the broad span of his thumb, a mesmerising caress that made it hard for her to think clearly. His touch was like a match to tinder, lighting spot fires all through her flesh, the molten heat stirring her pulse into overdrive.

'I know how cheesy this is going to sound, especially from me, but I can't think of a person I've enjoyed being with more than you,' Jack said, holding her gaze.

Sylvie had to remind herself Jack was a polished and practised playboy. He knew all the moves, memorised all the smooth lines that fed a woman's ego. She was cynical and jaded, so why should she feel a tingle of excitement at his comment? It was madness to believe anything he said. So many women had walked the road she was currently on with him. Soon that road would come to an end. She was surprised it hadn't already ended. Neither of them wanted the fairy tale. Neither of them wanted forever. They were only interested in each other for now.

Sylvie picked up her wine glass with her free hand and gave him a slanted smile. 'Nice try, Jack, for a moment there I thought you were going to say you'd fallen madly in love with me.'

This time the silence was so intense Sylvie heard one of the petals fall from the rose on the table and land on the starched linen tablecloth.

Jack was looking at her strangely, his expression grave yet confused at the same time. There was a frown pleating his brow, a shadow lurking in the back of his ice-blue eyes and an unusual set to his mouth. He slowly leaned back in his chair, his hand releasing hers. 'Is that what you want me to do? Fall in love with you?' His voice held no trace of emotion, it was almost robotic.

Sylvie gave a tinkle of laughter to cover her own confusion over her feelings about him. 'Relax, Jack. I'm here for a good time, not a long time.'

'Good to know,' Jack said with a smile that for once didn't match his eyes.

But Sylvie couldn't stop her thoughts drifting to a scenario where there wasn't a clock ticking on their time together. The more time she spent with Jack Wilde, the more she realised she had only known a certain version of him, the version he wanted people to see, not the real Jack.

The Jack Wilde who was sensitive and deep, who cared about his brothers even though he claimed they weren't close. The Jack who loved and respected his grandmother for all the sacrifices she had made to bring up him and his brothers after they were tragically orphaned. There were so many layers to the man she'd thought of as arrogant and overly confident.

He was still arrogant and confident and ridiculously privileged, but he was also a complex and deeply layered man. She had vastly underestimated his sensitivity, his generosity and kindness to those less fortunate than him, and the lengths he went to keep his philanthropy anonymous.

Sylvie had spent the last three or four years telling herself she hated Jack Wilde but now she was struggling to define her emotions. Struggling to accept the change in her feelings. Struggling to acknowledge the heartbreak she was setting herself up for if she were to reveal those feelings to Jack. How could life be so cruel as to make her fall in love with a man who could not return it? Her father had loved and left her and she had never seen or heard from him since. How could she be sure it wouldn't be the same with Jack Wilde? It was better to keep her feelings to herself, to squash them, to smother them rather than let them out to leap and dance with joyful anticipation only to have them dashed upon the rocks of reality.

After dinner, Jack took Sylvie to a nightclub where the music was a mix of modern, jazz and slow sexy ballads they could dance to. He longed to take her back to the hotel and make love to her but dancing with her was the best foreplay he had ever experienced. She moved in his arms as if they were in perfect sync, their bodies flush against each other, his erogenous zones firing up with incendiary heat sending his pulse sky high. He could feel his body stirring against her, the hot flow of blood urgent, desperate, hungry for satiation.

He was expecting his lust for her to have faded by now, to have at least lost its edge, but if anything, it had heightened, grown to a full-throttle force that was increasing every time he made love with her. He was finding it confusing to define how he felt about her. Lust was the first feeling but underneath that, something else was growing like tiny shoots pushing up through the cold winter's earth in search of warmth and sunshine. He tried to ignore them, to tread on them to stop them developing any further, but every now and again, something Sylvie would say or do would make those shoots push through his defences.

He didn't want to fall in love with anyone, not even someone as smart and sassy and entertaining as Sylvie Rathbone. There was so much he admired about her. She was a rag-to-riches tale of success and he couldn't help but admire her for it. So many people couldn't rise above disadvantage but she had. It said a lot about her determination, her drive, her grit and focus, which in a strange way reminded him of his own, although their childhood circumstances could not have been more different. He had checked his privilege long ago. He knew he was lucky compared to most, notwithstanding the tragic loss of his parents.

Jack slid his hand down the slender curve of her spine, holding her close to his throbbing need. 'Whose idea was it to go dancing?' he said with a wry smile.

She gave a tinkling bell laugh that made his blood sing. 'Yours, I believe. Are you in a hurry or something?'

'Or something,' he muttered, pulling her even closer.

She moved against him like a sensual cat and he had to smother a groan of longing. 'I never used to like dancing until I met you,' she said.

'I like dancing with you too,' Jack said, swirling her around to avoid another couple who were getting too close. 'You've only stepped on my toes three times.'

Sylvie laughed again and his chest swelled like a party balloon. 'Liar.'

'Or maybe it was four.'

She linked her arms around his neck and gazed into his eyes, her nutmeg-brown eyes shining. 'What have you got planned for us after this?'

Jack turned her again in his arms, enjoying the way her body moved with his in perfect unison. 'Can't you guess?'

She tilted her head to one side as if deep in thought. 'A nightcap somewhere cosy and romantic and then back to the hotel to bed to make love until the wee hours.'

Jack grinned down at her. 'Should I be worried you're able to read my mind?'

Sylvie gave a twisted smile. 'I'd be more worried if you could read mine.'

'Why?'

There was a beat or two of silence before she answered.

'Because it was easier to hate you before I spent any time getting to know you.' There was a note of worry in her voice and her smile had faded.

Jack tipped up her chin with his index finger, locking his gaze on hers. 'Let's not let our feelings get out of hand, Sylvie. We're having a good time together but that doesn't mean we're taking this further than a fun fling.'

'I never said I wanted more than a fun fling.' Her tone was defensive and her gaze sharpened. 'I'm just saying I don't hate you anymore. Or would you prefer it if I did?'

'No, of course not.' The last thing Jack wanted was Sylvie to loathe him. He was enjoying their time together too much. He had definitely enjoyed the spark of animosity she brought to their relationship at the start but now he liked the fact he could talk to her as an equal. Although their backgrounds were so disparate, their work ethic and drive to succeed were the same. He had not experienced such a connection with anyone else before, but he was wary of labelling it anything other than appreciation and respect of her on every level.

He found her forthrightness about what she wanted refreshing. She had been upfront right from the start about not wanting the fairy tale ending or expecting any sort of commitment from him. She was a career woman with no plans for settling down with a husband or partner.

It should have made him feel relieved but instead it made him feel inexplicably agitated. He kept coming back to it like his tongue would do to a sore tooth. It kept niggling at him but he couldn't understand why. He was a playboy who valued his freedom above all else. But he was enjoying this temporary relationship with Sylvie and wasn't in a hurry to end it anytime soon.

But he would end it.

CHAPTER ELEVEN

A FEW DAYS after they returned from Paris, Sylvie's mother invited herself and her new partner over to dinner. On one hand Sylvie was pleased her mother was moving on with her life, and she was certainly interested in meeting the man who had pulled her mother out of a twenty-two-year dating hiatus, but on the other she was disappointed because she had hoped to spend the evening with Jack. She hadn't seen him since they had got back, because his grandfather had experienced a fall, and Jack went down to Wildewood to help his grandmother organise yet another carer for him. Since his stroke the year before, Maxwell had gone through several carers so far, his irascible temper sending six—at last count—packing with haste to leave, no matter how wonderful the pay and free board at the grand estate.

Before her mother was due to arrive, Sylvie took out some food for Shadow. She had left a self-feeding container of dry food for the little cat while she was away for the weekend with Jack and she was relieved to see it wasn't quite empty, so at least Shadow hadn't gone hungry. To her surprise, she found Shadow waiting for her in the shrubbery, her wide green eyes focussed with intensity on her.

'Hi, Shadow,' Sylvie cooed. 'Here's your dinner. I bought a smoked salmon mornay for you. I hope you like it.'

The little cat crouched lower, hesitancy in her eyes and body but after a moment or two, she took a couple of cautious steps closer to the dish of food. Sylvie stayed stock-still, as still as her tiny angel statue to the left of her colourful and fragrant potted plants. Paw by paw, the small cat came closer, her body crouched low to the ground, her eyes wary, guarded. But the delicious smell of the food must have been a strong inducement because Shadow overcame her wariness and moved closer to the dish.

Sylvie held her breath, silently praying the little cat would trust her enough to eat in her presence. She suddenly realised her relationship with Shadow was not unlike her one with Jack. She had been wary of him at first, avoidant and reluctant to develop any feelings for him other than dislike. Was it fear that had held her back? *Hate* was such a strong and toxic word and now she couldn't associate it at all with her feelings for him.

She didn't want to admit to anything deeper than a satisfying physical and intellectual connection that was better than anything she had experienced with anyone before but…love? How could she allow herself to fall in love with an emotionally unavailable man? So many of her clients had made the same mistake, repeating patterns and scripts from their childhood.

Sylvie was particularly aware of the danger she

could be in because of the impact of her parents' divorce and the sudden cessation of her father's love and how that had affected her as a small, bewildered child. Although she was fully cognisant that knowledge didn't necessarily change behaviour, at least she had awareness of the danger of pursuing an unavailable man and there was no more unavailable man than the prince of all playboys—Jack Wilde.

Sylvie was so inside her head she hadn't noticed Shadow had finally closed the distance and was eating the food, all the while keeping a cautious eye on Sylvie. The sense of victory Sylvie felt was so satisfying and she couldn't wait to tell Jack. But then she reminded herself Jack was not her go-to person to share every mundane or important thing that happened in her life. He was her temporary fling partner, and frankly, she was surprised he hadn't ended their involvement by now. By his standards, it was a long fling and she knew it couldn't last much longer, even though deep down she wished it could.

Not forever…just for a little longer.

Sylvie waited until Shadow had eaten more than half the food before she reached out her hand and tentatively stroked the little cat's fur. Shadow flinched but surprisingly didn't run away. Sylvie waited a few seconds and stroked her again, long, slow gentle strokes that reminded her of Jack's bone-melting caresses.

There was a familiar sound of Jack's bifold doors opening next door and Shadow froze, then dashed out of sight to the back of the garden. Sylvie rose from her squatting position and faced Jack, who had come to the fence to speak to her.

'Guess what?' She couldn't keep the excitement out of her voice. So what if Jack wasn't her go-to person, she had to share her victory over being close enough to stroke Shadow and since her mother and new partner hadn't arrived yet, at least she could tell her neighbour.

'What?'

'I stroked Shadow!'

'Wow. And she didn't scratch you?' There was a hint of concern in his tone and expression.

'No, but she heard you opening your doors and bolted.'

'Sorry to interrupt your petting session but I wanted to see you,' Jack said, hopping the fence before she had a chance to tell him she was expecting dinner guests any minute now.

He came over to her and leaned down to press a lingering kiss to her mouth. She opened her lips to the commanding stroke of his tongue and his arms came around her, and she nestled closer, the kiss deepening with passion so hot it made her bones threaten to melt like heated honey. Jack groaned with satisfaction and brought one of his hands up to splay his fingers through her hair, evoking a whimper of delight from her. No one had ever kissed her with the spine-tingling expertise of Jack Wilde. She craved the taste of him, the sensual contours of his lips were branded on her own. She knew she would never forget his kiss, his touch, his lovemaking no matter how many years passed.

Jack finally lifted his mouth off hers to gaze down

at her, his hands now cupping her face. 'So, tell me about Shadow. You really got close enough to pat her?'

Sylvie found herself smiling widely, her voice as excited as a child's. 'I did and it was amazing. She let me stroke her a couple of times. And look how close to my back door I'm feeding her now.' She pointed to the almost empty dish on the flagstones near the potted plants.

'Well done, you.' Jack planted another quick kiss to her lips.

Sylvie was about to return the kiss when she heard her doorbell ring. It was one that rang through to her phone, which was in her back pocket.

'Are you expecting someone?' There was a thread of something she hadn't heard in Jack's voice before and his smiling expression was exchanged for a frowning one.

'It's my mother and her new partner,' Sylvie said, taking out her phone and then addressing her mother via the video function. 'Hi, Mum, I'm just out back. I'll be there in a second to let you in.'

'I'd better let you get on with your evening.' Jack made a half turn before Sylvie put her hand out and caught him by the forearm.

'Jack, please stay. I'm meeting my mother's new partner for the first time and I'm a little nervous to be honest. I don't want to spoil this for her but what if I don't like him? You're a good judge of character. Would you mind joining us for dinner?'

'Aren't you worried about keeping our…association a secret?'

'It's my mum. She won't tell anyone if I ask her not to.'

He seemed to give it some thought before answering, a frown still carved in between his blue eyes. 'Okay. So, how do we play this? We're lovers, colleagues or just friendly neighbours?'

Sylvie shifted her lips from side to side, trying to decide what approach was best. 'Let's go with the friendly neighbours for now.'

He hesitated for another nanosecond before responding. 'Okay.'

Sylvie beckoned him to follow her and she went back inside her house to let her guests in the front door.

As soon as she opened the door, Sylvie saw the marked difference in her mother's appearance. Linda Rathbone had a new shorter and fuller hairstyle, and she was wearing flattering makeup, including lipstick and eyeshadow that highlighted the sparkle of happiness in her gaze. It was like looking at a different person than the drab and lonely figure Sylvie was so used to seeing.

'Hi, Mum,' Sylvie began but she was swept up in a squishy hug by her mother that threatened to crack one or two of her ribs.

'Oh, darling, it's so wonderful to see you,' Linda said, then letting Sylvie go, turned to the gentleman standing a step behind her. 'This is Patrick McLaughlin, my fiancé.'

'Fiancé?' Sylvie blurted in shock, her eyes so wide the late evening sunlight seemed too bright.

Linda stuck out her hand where a gorgeous engagement ring blinked and glittered with brilliance. 'As of this morning. It was so romantic. Patrick asked me at the garden centre where we first met. Wasn't that sweet of him?'

Sylvie quickly remembered her manners and put out her hand to her mother's fiancé. 'It's so lovely to meet you, Patrick. And…erm, congratulations.'

'It's lovely to meet you too,' Patrick said with a warm smile that matched his grey eyes. 'Your mother has told me so much about you.'

Linda's eyes suddenly homed in on the tall figure standing to the left of Sylvie's shoulder. 'Oh, is this… Jack Wilde?'

Sylvie's first thought: How the flipping heck did her mother recognise Jack? The second: Why did I invite Jack to stay? Her mother would think she was dating him and then there'd be talk of future grandkids and Sylvie would have to remind her mum she was a fully signed-up career woman who had no interest in the fairy tale and family gig.

And yet…a part of her mind pictured a future with Jack. Jack waiting for her at the end of the aisle of a church. Jack stroking her swollen belly, with a proud smile on his handsome face. Jack helping her through the agony and ecstasy of labour. Jack holding a tiny red-faced bundle in his arms, his blue eyes moist with tears of joy and pride and love.

Sylvie shook herself out of her stasis and brought herself back to the moment. 'Oh yes, Jack is my new neighbour. Jack, this is my mother, Linda, and her fiancé, Patrick.'

Jack reached out his hand to each of them, warmly greeting them both. 'So nice to meet you. Congratulations on your engagement. When's the big day?'

Linda's eyes threatened to outshine the diamond glittering on her left hand. 'That's what we wanted to talk to Sylvie about tonight.' She shifted her sparkling gaze to her daughter. 'We don't want to wait for months and months—it's ridiculous at our age, so we thought sooner rather than later.'

Sylvie was aware she was frowning instead of smiling and tried to relax her tight expression, but her worries about her mother rushing into a second marriage made her tense and uneasy. 'How soon?'

'Next month,' Patrick said, smiling affectionately at his bride-to-be.

Linda beamed up at him, and Sylvie saw Patrick squeeze her mother's hand, his eyes full of love and admiration for his future wife.

Sylvie was finding it hard to think of something to say. She didn't feel comfortable encouraging a hasty marriage and yet she was glad her mother had found a seemingly lovely man after twenty-two years on her own. Who was she to spoil her mother's happiness? Life was short and her mum had wasted a lot of it already. How could Sylvie deny her this special moment in her life?

'I seem to be gatecrashing a family evening,' Jack said. 'I'll leave you to discuss the wedding with Sylvie.'

'Oh, please don't leave,' Linda said. 'At least Patrick will have someone to talk to while we girls talk wedding stuff.'

Sylvie wanted to sink beneath the floor. She was not the discuss-wedding-stuff type. She had never gazed longingly at the wedding dress displays in bridal boutiques. She had never looked at diamond rings in jewellery shop windows. She had never thought about walking up the aisle of a church or a wedding venue… until recently. Very recently. Scarily recently.

And she had to stop thinking about it because she knew Jack wasn't thinking along those lines at all and never would. She was being foolish for allowing her feelings to get involved in their fling. Flings and feelings didn't go together, or at least that was what she had fooled herself into believing.

'No, please stay, Jack,' Sylvie found herself saying, thinking that at least she would have someone to debrief with once her mother and Patrick left.

'If you're sure?' Jack was nothing if not polite.

Sylvie smiled until she thought her face would crack. 'I'm sure.'

Dinner was a surprisingly convivial affair, although Sylvie wondered why she was so surprised given she already knew how charming Jack could be. He made the dinner party flow with lively conversation and he drew out the more reserved nature of Patrick with consummate ease. Once the main meal was over, Sylvie and her mother headed to the kitchen to assemble a dessert Sylvie had prepared earlier. Jack and Patrick wandered outside so Jack could get some landscaping advice from Patrick, who was a keen gardener. Sylvie suspected Jack was giving her the space to talk to her mother and it made her feelings for him grow all the more.

A few weeks ago, she would never have considered Jack a sensitive man and yet the more time she spent with him the more she realised he was not just intellectually intelligent, but highly emotionally and socially intelligent, qualities she deeply admired. And with his razor-sharp wit and dry humour he was everything a woman wanted. The crazy thing was, she hadn't known *she* wanted it. Wanted him.

'So, tell me about Jack,' Linda said, giving Sylvie a twinkling eyed look.

'We're neighbours and colleagues and…friends.' She could have kicked herself for hesitating over the word *friends* but she'd realised he wasn't just a lover, he was indeed a friend, not the enemy she had always thought him to be.

'Friends with benefits?' Linda asked.

Sylvie could feel her cheeks heating. She had never discussed her dating life with her mother because of her mother's lack of one. She hadn't wanted to make her mum feel even worse about her aching loneliness after the divorce from Sylvie's father. But everything had changed now. Her mother was engaged and clearly had a loving and satisfying physical relationship with Patrick, judging by the affectionate touches and looks she had witnessed between them during the evening.

'I don't quite know how to describe my relationship with Jack,' Sylvie said, absently handing her mother a washed punnet of strawberries to hull. She dried her hands on some kitchen paper and continued. 'I never used to like him. I found him arrogant and way too self-assured and he's so wealthy and privileged it's ridiculous, but he moved in next door and I started to get to know him more.'

'And?' her mother prompted, her eyes expectant, hopeful.

'And we see each other from time to time but he's a playboy and I'm a career woman, so there's no future in it.'

'Are you sure?'

Sylvie slid a cheesecake closer to her mother to decorate with the strawberries. 'Can anyone be sure about how relationships will go? I'd like to know more about Patrick and why you're in such a hurry to marry him, especially when you married my father within months of meeting him. How can you be sure you're not making the same mistake?'

Linda met Sylvie's concerned gaze with a confident and assured look in her own. 'I know Patrick loves me and I love him, whereas I was never sure of your father's love. He was hot and cold towards me but the hot times were so good, they kept me tied to him for far longer than they should have.

'I'm older and wiser now. I've spent a long time on my own and I've done a lot of reflecting on why I was so biddable and accommodating with your father. He controlled me like a string puppet. I am Patrick's equal and we enjoy a very different dynamic. I want you to experience that too.'

'Oh, Mum, you know how important my career is to me.'

'I do but what about when you're my age or older? When you retire? Is it going to be as satisfying and rewarding then? Life isn't just about work. I understand some people enjoy solitude and their own space but I worry your lack of interest in relationships is my fault.'

Sylvie made a business of wiping away a tiny crumb from the cheesecake base off the serving dish. 'It's not your fault at all.'

'The divorce hit me hard, darling, but I see now how much harder it hit you. You didn't just lose your father and your home; you lost the mother you needed. I was so broken by his betrayal I didn't recognise how my depression was affecting you. You had to be the adult, which no young child should ever have to be. I shouldn't have been so blind to what you were going through, but you always were good at masking your feelings, even as a tiny child. You witnessed things, arguments and shouting matches for instance, that made you shut down. I've read up on it recently. It's traumatic for young children to be in such a toxic environment. You didn't feel safe and I couldn't keep you safe. I'm glad now your father left. I can't believe I was so distraught when he did because I was the one who should have left him. But there weren't the supports around that there are today. I was also immature and too proud to ask for help.'

'You did your best, Mum. That's all anyone can do under such difficult circumstances.'

Linda put her arms around Sylvie and hugged her tightly. 'Don't mask your feelings for Jack if you have them. Be yourself with him, your real self. Patrick has helped me to understand showing vulnerability isn't a weakness, it's a strength.'

Sylvie hugged her mother back, delighted she had finally gained some insight, but she was left with a lot to think about herself. Was she masking her feelings for Jack? What exactly did she feel for him? Wasn't it just lust? A crush that would soon fade. A week or three of madness she would look back on one day as an enjoyable experience but nothing else. What else could it be?

Sylvie's mother and partner had not long left for their hotel when Jack said he too should go home and get some sleep.

'Wouldn't you like a nightcap?' Sylvie asked, trying to disguise the longing in her tone for more of his company.

He gave her one of his spine-tingling crooked smiles, the type of smile that made his eyes light up and sent her senses into free fall. 'Just the one.'

He insisted on helping her clear away the dinner things first, which to her seemed something way outside his experience having grown up with so much wealth—there was no doubt a staff member for every task at Wildewood, his family pile.

Sylvie gave him a sideways glance as he reached for the same plate as her, his fingers brushing hers, sending a shower of sparks exploding through her flesh. 'When did you become so domesticated?'

'I was in a share house during university. What an eye-opener that was.'

Sylvie stopped clearing the table to stare at him. 'A share house? With more than one person?'

'Yep. I even learned to cook.'

'Really?'

Jack took the plates she was holding, so he could load them in the dishwasher. 'I can't say I'm a gourmet chef or anything but I thought it was time I became a bit more independent.'

Sylvie followed him to the kitchen. 'Did you ever live with a partner?'

'No, I've never stayed with someone long enough for it to be a possibility.'

'Have you ever been in love?' Sylvie adopted a bland tone but she was intensely curious to know the answer. His lifestyle as a carefree playboy could have been borne out of having his heart broken at some stage.

Jack gave his bone-melting laugh. 'No, and nor do I intend to. What about you?'

Sylvie shook her head. 'I don't think I'm one of those people who falls in love easily. My married colleagues in the practice fell for each other the first time they kissed. I just can't imagine anyone impressing me *that* much.'

There was a weighted silence. Sylvie became aware of a different pressure in the air, a tightening, a thickening, a closing in feeling that felt like a spotlight was on her and Jack standing facing each other in her kitchen.

Jack's gaze lowered to her lips at the same time hers drifted to his. The silence pulsed with possibilities, tempting, dangerously erotic possibilities.

'It must have been a pretty awesome kiss.' His voice was husky as if he had gargled with gravel.

'Yes…' Sylvie swept the tip of her tongue out over her bone-dry lips, her eyes still trained on his mouth like a powerful magnet was holding them there. She could not move. Her feet were glued to the polished floor, her senses tingling with awareness of Jack's proximity. He was suddenly close enough to touch and yet she couldn't recall moving.

It was like being cast under some sort of spell, her body was on autopilot, her rational brain switched off. She could feel her body's primal response to his presence, the soft tug of her female flesh, the hollow ache between her legs, a thickening and moistening of her most secret place. Her heart rate rose, her breathing intervals changed, her willpower deserting her when she needed it most.

Jack reached out a hand and picked up a few strands of her hair and slowly coiled them around his index finger, his eyes never leaving hers. 'I was right,' he said, still with a husky tone that made the backs of her knees tingle.

'About what?' Sylvie could barely recognise her own voice; it was hardly more than a breathless thread of sound.

'Your hair is like silk.' He tightened the coil of hair he was holding a fraction and a hot tingle of need whispered down her spine. He lifted her hair to his nose and briefly closed his eyes as he breathed in the scent of her hair. 'Mmm…' He opened his eyes again and something dropped from a height in her belly. His eyes were mesmerising, the ice blue reminding her of an ocean, deep, mysterious, unfathomable.

Sylvie knew she should pull out of his intimate hold, knew she should put a stop to this spellbinding moment between them, but she couldn't seem to do it. Her body was running its own agenda, desperate to see what his intention was. Was he flirting with her? Was he going to kiss her? Should she allow it? Damn, she wanted him to. So badly it was an ache in her flesh.

Jack bent down so his mouth was just above hers, the breeze of his warm breath teasing her senses into a frenzy. 'You should stop me before I go any further.' His voice was as deep as organ pipes, a throb of sound that sent a wave of longing coursing through her body.

'Why should I stop you when I want you to go further?' Sylvie stared at his mouth so close to hers, studying the sculptured contours, the way his dark stubble was peppered along his jaw and chin and above his top lip in such a sexy manner. She had to keep her hands on the cool marble of the kitchen counter to stop them exploring his jaw, to feel the pinpricks of regrowth against the skin of her hands. She could smell the citrus notes of his aftershave that reminded her of a sunbaked lemon orchard, the base notes of wood and leather and something else which was as addictive as a mind-altering drug.

'Because the kitchen is a mess and we both have work in the morning, but I want to make love to you for hours.'

Sylvie shivered at his words, at his touch, at his promise of pleasure she could see in his glittering gaze.

'We both know this has to stop at some point, Jack.' She didn't want it to stop but she knew the longer it continued, the harder it would be for her to let go. She was aware of the danger she was drifting into…was already knee-deep in. She was falling for him and starting to dream about him as a life partner.

He frowned and placed his hands on her hips, holding her against his stirring body. 'No one has found out so far, apart from your mother and Patrick.'

She twisted her lips. 'My mother gave me a lecture about not letting work get in the way of living a full life.'

'A full life meaning marriage and kids?'

'She only wants me to be happy, to enjoy what she's got now after waiting so long for someone to love her.'

'But isn't what you want for your life the main thing you should be concerned about, not what your mother or whoever thinks?'

'Of course it's my decision, but you know what mothers are like.'

There was a heavy silence and then Sylvie realised her gaffe.

'I'm so sorry, Jack, you didn't have your mother long enough to really know how much she and your dad loved you.'

A shadow passed through his gaze like a cloud blocking the sun. 'I was old enough to know they loved me but I've lived ever since with the regret I didn't tell them I loved them before they died.' His deep voice contained a burden that was almost palpable and lines of sadness were etched in his expression. 'It's not that

I didn't have the opportunity. I just didn't see it as important.'

'I'm so sorry…' Words seemed so inadequate, platitudes he had no doubt heard for years but without giving any comfort.

He stared at her for a long moment as if studying her features, memorising them in minute detail so he never forgot how she looked once they ended their fling. 'Do you realise you are the only person, apart from my brother Jago, that I've confessed that to?' His voice was still ocean-floor deep and gravel-husky and his eyes contained a glimpse of raw emotion she had never seen in them before.

'That must be so painful for you to live with but I'm sure they wouldn't have thought you didn't love them. Some kids are just more open with their feelings than others.'

He gave an effigy of a smile. 'Did you ever love your father?'

Sylvie loathed talking of her childhood but it was only fair she shared with him now that he'd shared one of his deepest regrets. 'I adored him and he made me feel adored in return. But my parents divorced when I was ten and my father claimed he had no money to pay maintenance for me, so my mum and I were always moving to cheaper rentals, always trying to make ends meet. It was like he was punishing her even though he was the one to leave, not her.'

'Do you ever see him?'

Sylvie blew out a short breath. 'No, not since I was ten.' She twisted her mouth into an embittered grimace.

'He was one of those dads who said he loved me almost daily but then he left and I never heard it again. I don't trust those words now. They're so easy to say but how can you ever trust if they're genuine?'

Jack gave a nod of agreement but again something moved through his gaze, a shadow, a flicker, a feeling he was suppressing. 'Maybe it's actions you need to put your trust in, not words.'

'Maybe…'

He held her gaze for another long moment. 'I should let you get to bed. It's been a long evening but I really enjoyed meeting your mum and Patrick.'

'I can't help worrying she's rushing into marriage. What if he leaves her like my father did?'

Jack put his hands on the tops of her shoulders, gently squeezing them. 'There's always the chance a relationship might not work out but they seem well-suited and their personalities mesh well.' He bent down and pressed a barely touching kiss to her lips that made her hungry for more. She linked her arms around his neck and leaned into his warmth, aching for him with a primal need that pulsed through her with growing urgency.

Sylvie's phone began to ring on the kitchen bench and she tried to ignore it, but it was after eleven at night and if it wasn't a scam call then it might be Maria calling to let her know Natasha was in labour. 'Sorry, Jack, I'd better get this.' She slipped out of his hold and looked at the screen and saw it was indeed Mariah. 'Mariah? Is everything all right?'

'We're at the hospital now,' Mariah said, a thread of

worry in her voice. 'Natasha's in labour and it's happening faster than we expected. Can you come? I know it's late but we both could do with the support.'

'Of course, I'll come right away. Just text me the details and I'll jump in a ride-share now, so I don't have to worry about parking.'

'Thank you so much. We really wanted you to be there for the birth but we didn't realise she would go in a month early.'

'I'll be there soon.' Sylvie hung up and before she could say a word Jack had already taken his keys out of his trouser pocket.

'I'll drive you there now. I only had one glass of wine hours ago.'

'Oh, would you? That would be so lovely of you. My partners in the firm are having their first baby and they want me there for the birth.'

'I hope you've got the stomach for it. I've heard from my friend Ben that it can get pretty intense.'

'I can handle it,' Sylvie said, hoping it was true.

A few minutes later, Jack pulled up in front of the hospital's entrance, got out of the driver's side and opened Sylvie's door. Once she was out of the car, he leaned down to kiss her. 'Good luck. And thanks for dinner. It was amazing.'

'Bye.' Sylvie waved to him as she dashed off to the entrance of the hospital.

CHAPTER TWELVE

FORTY-FIVE MINUTES LATER, Sylvie sat by Natasha's delivery bed, holding the newborn Hamish Andrew in her arms. His tiny face was red and a bit scrunched up like a grumpy old man, but he was sound asleep and Sylvie marvelled at the miracle of birth. She had seen births on television but never in real time, in the delivery suite. The overwhelming emotions of it ambushed her and she found herself crying with a combination of joy, relief, happiness and a teensy-weensy bit of envy.

The envy aspect shocked her for she had not pictured herself as a mother, but holding this precious newborn in her arms and witnessing the love and pride of his parents, Natasha and Mariah, made her wonder if she had masked her maternal yearnings instead of owning them. Well, she was owning them now.

Hamish had a crop of reddish-brown hair but Sylvie began to imagine what Jack's baby would look like. Would it have a shock of ink-black hair like him and those amazing ice-blue eyes, or would the baby favour her? She had to pull herself away from her musings with an effort. She was being a romantic fool for thinking about a future with Jack Wilde.

She was not the romantic type. She didn't trust the fairy tale would deliver on its promise of a happy ending. She was a divorce lawyer; she knew the stats. She witnessed daily the fallout, the fights and fury, the devastation of people's lives who had once loved one another. She had lived experience of it with her own parents' divorce. Why, then, was she allowing herself to think of a happy ever after with Jack Wilde of all people?

Because Jack had done what she thought no one could do—make her fall in love. This was no passing crush or infatuation. This was not a casual fling—or at least not for her. This was the life-changing real deal. Her heart was full of love for Jack. How had he got through her armour? Her defences? She had built walls around her heart for as long as she could remember but Jack had melted them away the first time he'd held her in his arms at the masked ball. Something had changed in that moment. Something irreversible.

How could she have not realised it until now?

'Isn't he gorgeous?' Mariah said, still wiping at her own eyes after helping her partner through a fast and painful labour.

'He's divine,' Sylvie said, smiling down at the baby in her arms. 'But I'd better give him back to you before I get any crazy ideas.' Like becoming Jack's bride. Having his baby. Living a life of forever love with him. Crazy ideas she had no business thinking about because Jack wasn't a forever-love guy.

Mariah carefully took her son from Sylvie's arms and crooned to him, rocking him from side to side, the look on her face one of complete and utter devotion. The same love and devotion on Natasha's face in spite of her physical exhaustion.

Yep, Sylvie was envious and confused and angry with herself for getting mixed up with Jack Wilde in the first place. But how could she give him up? He hadn't mentioned anything about a timeline on their fling and nor had she. So far, only her mother and Patrick knew about their involvement, and of course Natasha and Mariah had guessed something was going on at their baby shower, but how long could Jack and Sylvie hope to keep it a secret from everyone else? What lengths would they have to go to?

Surely Jack would tire of it and move on. She was surprised he hadn't already done so. According to the tabloids, he normally didn't stay with a lover more than a day or two. But the Jack Wilde profiled in the tabloids was not the Jack Wilde she had fallen in love with in private. There was so much about Jack the public didn't know, and Sylvie was still finding out things about him and wanted to keep doing that—growing closer to him like she was doing with Shadow the stray cat, establishing a bond of trust.

After dropping Sylvie at the hospital, Jack drove home but he couldn't settle. Sleep was impossible. The evening felt unfinished, incomplete, left hanging…

He had expected to spend the night with Sylvie. He wanted to recreate the intimacy they had shared in Paris. He even called it the Paris Bubble. It was where they could both be themselves, not looking over their shoulder for the paparazzi to snap them together, not worrying about their clients thinking they were compromising their case. Their time in Paris had strengthened his desire for her rather than dialled it down.

He found himself thinking of her more than he thought of anything or anyone. He was becoming obsessed with her. He ached for her with every cell in his body, a hot burning desire he knew would only be satisfied by being with her. He wanted to feel her come apart in his arms. He loved the feel of her skin against his own. He longed to trail his fingers through the chestnut silk of her hair, to feel it tickle his skin as she draped herself over his naked body. He shuddered with the erotic memory of their passionate encounters. Was it the secrecy of their fling that was making him so obsessed with her? Was it the element of danger, the thrill of keeping their fling out of the public eye? He had never felt this way about a woman before. He wanted her like a drug. He was addicted to her touch, to the sound of her voice, to her tinkling bell laugh, her whip-quick wit and her soft brown eyes that melted the hardest core of him.

Jack opened his bifold doors and looked out over his yet-to-be-landscaped garden. After all the tradespeople and their equipment, his backyard was little more than a large square of mud apart from a lone Japanese maple tree. His chat with Patrick had been helpful and he was looking forward to having the garden completed. He watched out for Sylvie's little cat just as he did every day. The food he had put out earlier had been eaten but there was no sign of Shadow.

Jack pushed aside the feelings of loneliness. He

wasn't a lonely person. He never allowed himself to be. He kept busy. He worked and played hard. He had projects on the go that needed his attention. There were any number of mates he could call, even at this hour if he wanted company.

But the only company he wanted was Sylvie's.

He sat watching her house for hours but she didn't come home. He knew enough about labour from his mate Ben to know it wasn't a predictable affair, so Sylvie might not come home for ages yet or may even spend the night at the hospital with her friends. He fought down the desire to call or text her. He didn't want to interrupt what was one of the most significant events in her friends' lives. Once it got to three in the morning, he decided to go to bed but sleep was frustratingly elusive. He closed his eyes but all he could see in his mind was Sylvie smiling at something he'd said earlier in the evening. He loved the way her soft mouth lifted up at the corners and the shine in her eyes when she met his gaze.

Jack thumped his pillow and turned onto his back and stared at the ceiling. Why had he let this madness continue so long? He was wading into territory he had never ventured into before. The feelings territory. The territory he had cordoned off when he was a child after the loss of his parents. He had armoured up, frozen his shattered heart and soldiered on to survive.

He was not going to open that vault for anyone.

Sylvie arrived at work the following morning feeling a little sleep-deprived but glad she had been able to support her friends and colleagues through such an important time. Her secretary Samira looked up from her computer and after a quick chat about how gorgeous Hamish Andrew was, and after seeing Sylvie's photos on her phone, informed her Edwina Winters had booked an appointment with her at nine thirty that morning. 'She said it was urgent so I moved Nola Clarke to this afternoon. You had a gap for admin anyway.'

Sylvie tried not to show her frustration. Her two-hour admin gap was a way to catch up on client work so she didn't have to take so much paperwork home. There was never enough time to keep ahead of the paperwork in complicated cases but she always did her best. 'Okay. I'll see her but we might have to be a little firmer with her in future. I can't be flexible for her and not for anyone else.'

'I know,' Samira said with an apologetic look. 'But she's hard to say no to.'

'Yeah, and she's not the only one,' Sylvie muttered, and turned towards her office.

Sylvie had barely finished her coffee before Edwina Winters arrived, pushing open the office door and then closing it with a snap that made Sylvie stiffen in her chair.

Edwina's eyes were like two burning lamps and her normally pale complexion was pink with rage. 'I saw you last night,' she said through tight lips. 'I was at the hospital with Mimi. She needed stitches this time.'

Sylvie frowned in concern. 'Is she all right?'

'Yes, but that's not why I'm here.'

An icy shiver worked its way down the length of Sylvie's spine. 'Then why are you here?'

'I saw you with Jack Wilde.' Edwina's voice vibrated and her eyes flashed with venom. 'I saw him kiss you when he dropped you at the hospital. How could you do this to me? He's Hugo's lawyer and you've betrayed my trust by sleeping with the enemy.'

Sylvie disguised a convulsive swallow. She normally refused to discuss her private life with a client but she owed Edwina some sort of explanation. 'Jack and I are neighbours and friends. We've been on opposing sides of court cases before and no doubt will again. Our…association will have no bearing on my handling of your divorce. I am a professional and so is Jack.'

'I can't believe you've betrayed me like this.' Edwina was in full victim mode. 'I thought you were the one person I could trust.'

'You can trust me, Edwina,' Sylvie said. 'I will continue to do everything in my power to represent you and fight for you. You have my word.'

Edwina swiped at her eyes where tears had formed. 'I was so worried about Mimi last night…'

'Please…' Sylvie came around from her desk and patted one of the client's chairs. 'Sit down and tell me what happened.'

Edwina obediently sat, and Sylvie plucked a couple of tissues from the box on her desk and handed them to her. She then perched on the corner of her desk rather than go back behind it to her own chair.

'What happened?'

'Hugo called and insisted on talking to both the kids.

Mimi reluctantly spoke to him but apparently, he emotionally blackmailed her and then a couple of hours later, I found her in the bathroom with both wrists…' Edwina gulped as if recalling that terrifying scene was retraumatising her as it would have anyone. 'I'm not a nurse or a doctor or anything but I knew she needed stitches. I did what I could with a towel to stop the bleeding and took her in a taxi to the hospital. I was in the hospital café getting a drink for her when I saw you get out of Jack Wilde's car.'

'I'm so sorry you've had such an upsetting experience with Mimi. You must still be in shock. Is she okay? Has she had a mental health assessment?'

'Yes, the psychiatrist on duty assessed her and recommended she have some sessions with a psychologist but how am I going to afford it? Hugo refuses to pay for it. He doesn't believe in talk therapy. He just expects her to pull herself together.'

'A lot of people don't understand the benefit of therapy,' Sylvie said. 'Finding the right one is an issue, of course, but I'm sure one who specialises in adolescents will help Mimi through this difficult time. Right now, you're her best support and you're doing the best you can.'

Edwina was visibly less agitated by now and had stopped crying. She bundled the tissues into a ball and pushed them up the sleeve of her cardigan. 'Thank you. I'm sorry for barging in like this but I can't let Hugo destroy the children, especially Mimi. He can't see what he's doing to them. He refuses to see it. He thinks it's my fault they lack resilience but he's always tearing down their confidence.'

'Some people parent the way they were parented, and it can have devastating results,' Sylvie said. 'At least the children have you.'

A look of panic entered Edwina's gaze. 'But what if Hugo wins custody?'

Sylvie straightened her shoulders with steely determination. 'He's not going to win. I'll make sure of it.'

Sylvie was agitated for the rest of the day. It was near impossible to concentrate on her work because all she could think about was how her involvement with Jack may have compromised Edwina Winters's divorce case. She couldn't get over the shame of allowing herself to be tempted into his bed when he was the lawyer of her client's estranged husband. She should have known better. She was furious with her own weakness, at allowing herself to fall into Jack's bed when she had known all along the dangerous line she was walking. She was supposed to be focused on her work. On her client in a difficult divorce that involved traumatised children. The Winterses' children were at risk, especially Mimi. Mimi's cutting was a cry for help and if there was another episode it may be even more serious than the last one.

Finally, the long and arduous and emotionally draining day was over and she caught a ride-share so she could get home to speak to Jack in person. She dumped her briefcase and bag inside her front door, then locked it and went straight to Jack's house.

He answered the door just as she was reaching for the doorbell. 'Hey, I was just about to come over to see you. How did the delivery go?' His smile was wide and dangerously attractive.

Sylvie looked at him blankly for a moment. Her mind was so fixated on what she had to say to him, she couldn't for the life of her understand what he was referring to.

'The baby?' he prompted.

'Fine,' she said with a curt edge to her voice. 'I'm not here to talk about that. I need to talk to you.'

'Come in.' He waved her in and she stalked past him with her head held high, desperately trying not to notice the alluring scent of his aftershave, or the way his rich dark stubble gave his mouth and jawline such sexy appeal. Damn the man for being so handsome and irresistible. He had caused her to compromise her standards and she had to stop imagining herself in love with him and tell him what she really thought of him.

Sylvie went as far as the sitting room, knowing she wouldn't be staying long. She folded her arms across her body and met his gaze. 'Edwina Winters saw us last night.'

Jack frowned. 'Saw us where?'

'When you dropped me off at the hospital. She was there with Mimi who had cut herself again.'

'Is Mimi okay?'

Sylvie was impressed he at least showed concern about the teenager first but it still didn't redeem him in her eyes. 'She had to have stitches but she's okay or at least until the next time. Your client is destroying his kids and he refuses to see it. He emotionally blackmails them and Mimi can't handle it.'

Jack's frown deepened. 'Look, personally I don't like the guy but—'

'I'm not interested in your opinion of him. What I want to know is did you sleep with me to compromise my case?'

Jack's expression locked down but she caught a glimpse of something that looked like hurt flicker through his gaze before his eyes turned to ice. 'Seriously? You think I would sink that low?'

Sylvie hitched up her chin, her righteous indignation in full lava flow. 'I can't help feeling you viewed me as a challenge to win over. You knew I didn't like you, so you made me fall…into bed with you.' She only just caught herself in time before letting slip she had fallen in love with him. 'I should never have allowed it to happen but—'

'Good to know you're accepting some responsibility for it.' His tone was sardonic, his expression as cold and hard as marble.

'How long were you going to let it continue?' Sylvie asked. 'Until we got all the way to court? Was this all a game to you? You thought it amusing to not only battle it out in court but to bed me in private?'

His jaw was like stone and a hard glint came into his eyes. 'Clearly nothing I say will stop you believing the worst of me but I genuinely wanted you.'

'So, you got me like you always get what you damn well want.' Sylvie was furious for allowing herself to fall into his arms just like every other woman who had come before her. And no doubt like everyone who would come after her. She was just a number on his long list of casual lovers. How could she have not seen it coming? Why had she caved in to his charms when she should have known better?

'I don't always get what I want,' Jack said, his posture still rigid like he was wearing an invisible suit of armour. 'Why is this such a big deal for you? It was just sex, remember? That's what you kept insisting it was and only ever could be.'

It was not comfortable being hoisted with one's own petard but now Sylvie was feeling the full spectrum of discomfort at having her own words thrown back at her. She had insisted their fling was a no-feelings, no-strings one. She had thought she could be a female version of Jack, having fun without feelings, but there was a price to pay and she was paying it now. 'Whatever it was, Jack, it's over now,' Sylvie said with an iron thread of determination in her voice. 'It was fun while it lasted but it's over.'

Jack scratched at his jaw as if he had been bitten by an insect. 'Is that what you want?'

Of course, it wasn't what she wanted but how could she tell him what her real desire was? Their affair had to end. It had no future and she had known it from the start but had gone ahead and fallen for him anyway. Her heart ached like it was being pulled apart in her chest. She straightened her spine and craned her neck to meet his gaze. 'I want to represent my client without any complications from being involved with her estranged husband's lawyer. I can't act for her to my best ability with you in my private life.'

'We weren't committing a crime, Sylvie. It was just sex between two consenting adults.' His casual attitude to what they had shared shredded what hope she had clung to that he had somehow developed feelings for her.

Sylvie made a move to leave but Jack stepped in front of her. 'I didn't use you to distract you from the case. I don't want us to part with you thinking of me like that.' His tone was heavy with gravitas, his eyes steady and serious on hers.

'Oh, you have some regard for what I think of you, then, do you? I thought your devil-may-care attitude was across all areas of your life.' Sylvie saw him flinch as if she had slapped him but her sarcasm was her only way to protect herself from falling back into his arms. She knew she was projecting her anger at herself on him but it was the only way she could break things off with him. She had to use her anger as a shield, as her armour.

'We had a good time together, Sylvie. I don't regret a moment of it. And to quote a famous film, "*At least we'll always have Paris.*"'

Now it was Sylvie's turn to flinch but she was careful enough to do it on the inside. His words were like a sucker punch to her heart. How on earth did he know one of her favourite films of all time was the bittersweet romantic classic *Casablanca*? Their trip to Paris was not something she was going to forget anytime soon.

Sylvie stepped past him but this time he didn't stop

her. She walked out of his house and didn't look back. She wanted to. Desperately. But there was no turning back on her decision to end their fling. Jack didn't feel anything but lust for her and she refused to cheapen herself, to rob herself of the love she knew deep down she deserved.

Jack's front door snicked closed and he let out a breath he wasn't aware he'd been holding. Sylvie's words were still spooling through his brain like ticker tape having a tantrum. He was so blindsided by her decision to end their fling he couldn't get his thoughts into any working order. But it wasn't just his thoughts that were spinning out of control—it was having an effect on his body. His chest ached as if an anvil was tied to the bottom of his heart, dragging it down, down, down. Every breath he took hurt, every movement he made sent shock waves of pain through his body. Seeing Sylvie and not being able to touch her was a form of torture. He'd been looking forward to spending the evening together but instead she had ended their relationship.

Why was that such a big deal for him?

Jack drew in a deep breathe then released it in a whoosh of frustration. A hint of Sylvie's perfume lingered in the air as if to taunt him. He went to the kitchen and living area but fought against the desire to look at her house to see if he could see her. What was wrong with him? He wasn't a lovesick teenager with raging hormones. He was an adult in full control of his emotions.

He was always ahead of the game in flings. He had

never had anyone pull the plug on a relationship before now. Was that why he was feeling so… What *was* he feeling? He was so used to smothering his feelings before they took hold, he didn't even know how to describe what he was feeling right now. It was a combination of shock, anger and frustration. And yet there was more deep down inside him but he didn't want to open the vault. The lock on his heart was rusted in place and he was not going to prise it open.

So what if their fling ended? It had been fun while it lasted. Loads of fun. The best fun he'd had in ages… possibly ever. But he would find another lover soon enough. Jack was a playboy by choice. He made sure his life didn't have room for anything but no-strings relationships. Yes, he was cynical about relationships even though he had friends like Ben who were happily married. And soon his brother Jago would be married to Mollie, whether or not Jonas came home in time.

Jack had no right to be feeling let down and lost and…he flinched at the thought…lonely.

No. He wasn't the lonely type. He refused to think about the word, let alone feel the emotion.

CHAPTER THIRTEEN

SYLVIE THREW HERSELF into work and fortunately there was plenty of it to distract her from her feelings about Jack. The numerous divorce cases she was handling should have helped convince her she had done the right thing in ending their fling. Relationships failed so often, so bitterly and often vengefully and it didn't seem to matter what time length they had endured. One of her clients had been married fifty-one years, another only five months. Sylvie should be grateful that at least she had ended her fling with Jack without too much collateral damage. Or at least, not the sort you could see on the surface. But inside she was aching like she had some sort of cancer eating away at her flesh, gnawing away at her hopes and dreams, leaving her raw and sore and empty.

Coming home in the evenings was fraught with the worry of running into Jack getting out of his car or seeing him moving about in his house next door. She tried not to glance in his direction but her eyes veered that way no matter how hard she fought the urge. For the first couple of weeks, she saw no lights come on at night, so she imagined he was off dating another lover and spending the nights in hotels or perhaps visiting his grandparents. Sylvie had seen a photo of his family home Wildewood and was disappointed she hadn't got to see it in person. But then, how could she have done so while their fling had to remain a secret?

It hurt to think of him moving on so quickly with his playboy ways. It pained her to imagine his hands stroking someone else's body, his sensual mouth kissing someone else's lips. It was a form of torture to think about him at all, let alone being intimate with someone other than her. She was furious with herself for allowing herself to fall in love with him. Why couldn't she shut off her feelings?

Was she going to be like her mother, living years without moving on? Stuck on loving and missing an emotionally unavailable man? Jack was never going to be the I-love-you-forever type. The loss of his parents had made him lock away his feelings so he couldn't be hurt by them. She had done much the same, but somehow Jack had stormed through her defences with his charm and playful nature. From the first moment they danced together she knew she was in danger, so she had only herself to blame. She knew about his reputation. She knew he would never fall in love, because he was having too much fun living life as a billionaire playboy. Why had she thought for a nanosecond he might fall in love with her?

At least Sylvie had her mother's wedding to look forward to this weekend. Her mother and Patrick were getting married in Surrey in Patrick's large garden. Linda had invited Sylvie to come and stay for a few days before the wedding to help her prepare. The irony of the situation didn't escape Sylvie. It was usually the other way around—the mother would be helping the adult daughter prepare for her wedding.

But that was yet another silly thought Sylvie had to shut down. There was no point in thinking about Jack waiting for her down the aisle or petal strewn garden path. That was wishful thinking and it was a complete and utter waste of time.

Jack managed to fill his time with an unusually heavy workload but he relished the distraction. He wouldn't allow himself to think about Sylvie, because every time he did, he sank into a deep pit of loneliness that tortured him into a restless lack of focus during the day and sleeplessness at night. His usual defences were not operating at full capacity. He thought of her way more than he should have but he figured it was because he was bitter and resentful about her ending their fling, not him. Immature of him, sure, but a man had his pride and he was born and bred and bathed with it.

Jack hadn't seen Sylvie for a couple of weeks but then he received a text message from her asking him to feed Shadow as she was going to be away in Surrey for a few days at her mother and Patrick's wedding this coming weekend. The wording was polite and brief and no one reading it would have thought that they had ever shared an intimate relationship, and certainly not one that made Jack feel so out of sorts now it had ended.

Jack came home after another long day at work and, shrugging off his jacket, flung it over the back of one of the kitchen stools. He loosened his tie and tossed it in the same direction of his jacket. He sent his splayed fingers through his hair, letting out a long, weary sigh. He glanced at his phone but then in a fit of pique deleted every single dating app. It was an act of defiance but directed at whom he wasn't quite sure. Himself? A self-punishment? A time out in the wilderness of loneliness to teach him a lesson about not being so off his guard that he could be blindsided again? It was all of those things and more. He needed time and space to think. He was so used to moving on to the next lover, the next exciting temptation that caught his eye.

But no one caught his eye. He only had eyes for Sylvie Rathbone and it was driving him crazy. He had to move past this disappointment, this bewildering emptiness that was consuming him.

Jack got a tin of cat food out of his pantry and pulled the tab to open it. He unlocked his bifold doors and slid them open and went out to the still non-existent garden. Compared to Sylvie's lush and fragrant garden next door, his looked like a wasteland, which was kind of like his life right now. Empty, a shell of his former self, a wreck that needed considerable work to get it into some sort of positive shape.

There was a movement at the back corner of his block and he braced himself for encountering a rat, but relief swept through him when he saw it was Sylvie's little stray cat. She gave him a wary look with her green eyes, then crept slowly towards him. Jack bent down and put the cat food down in front of him, hoping the enticing smell of salmon would overcome her fear of contact.

'Hey, Shadow,' he said in a soft voice.

The little cat blinked at him and then gave a squeaky-sounding meow as if she was greeting him. Then to his surprise and considerable delight, Shadow came closer and began to eat the food he'd put in front of him.

Jack said, letting out a long sigh, 'I hope you like the salmon. I was going to give you the chicken one but variety is the spice of life…or so I used to think.'

Shadow looked up at him between mouthfuls and blinked at him, then went back to eating her dinner.

'I had a cat once, a long time ago,' Jack said, thinking back to his early childhood. 'But when she died a year or two after my parents, my grandfather refused to replace her. Her name was Miffy, like in the kids' books. I really missed her but I didn't tell anyone, not even my brothers. I guess I got used to keeping what I felt to myself.'

Shadow had finished most of the food and looked up at him again but this time she came closer to him and meowed again, louder this time, her green eyes looking straight into his. Jack blinked back a sudden build-up of moisture in his own eyes and swallowed against a walnut-sized lump in his throat. He slowly reached out his hand and gently stroked the little cat's coat, long slow strokes that she seemed to welcome for he heard her begin to purr. He blinked a couple of times to clear his watery vision and kept stroking the cat, talking to her in a gentle tone. 'Hey, you like that, huh? And here, behind the ears? Miffy used to love a scratch there too.'

Shadow continued to purr and then she turned and bumped her head against his hand as if to ask for more. Jack smiled, a warm feeling spreading throughout his chest like a flow of melted treacle. 'It looks like we're going to be friends after all,' he said, still stroking Shadow. 'You trust me now, huh? Good to know I still have it with the ladies.' He let out a long sigh. What a waste of a skill when he only wanted one lady—Sylvie.

The little cat stopped and blinked at him again. *Mee-oow.* This time her meow was stretched out as if she were trying to communicate something to him.

'You miss her too, huh?' Jack said. 'She's only away for the weekend but it feels like months to me.'

Meow.

Jack stroked his hand over Shadow's back and the little cat arched her spine in delight. 'Listen, I want to make a deal with you. If you're going to hang around you have to promise me something. No rats left on my doorstep, okay? I freaking hate the things.'

Shadow blinked innocently at him. *Meow.*

He straightened and, instead of shying away at his sudden movement, Shadow wove sinuously around his ankles, purring loudly. He looked down at her and gave a rueful smile. 'Oh, and there's another thing we have to get straight right from the get-go. If you want to come inside, fine. But under no circumstances do I want you on my bed.'

Prrrhht, Shadow said.

* * *

The following morning Jack had a scheduled meeting with Hugo Winters. Before Hugo could get into one of his rants about his estranged wife, Edwina, Jack took control of the session.

'Hugo, sit. I want to hear about what happened with Mimi a couple of weeks back.'

Hugo sat and then shifted his bulk in his chair as if no part of it was comfortable, his ruddy complexion darkening. 'That girl is too sensitive. Can't take any feedback. How is she going to survive university and the real world? She needs some backbone but her mother indulges her, gives in to her all the time. It's called enabling or codependence or—'

'It's called being a concerned parent, Hugo,' Jack said. 'Do you realise you could have lost your daughter that night?'

Hugo made a snorting noise. 'She was play-acting. It's attention-seeking, as I've said right from the start.'

'What sort of attention do you give her? Positive or negative?' Jack was thinking of his own childhood and his overly critical grandfather and how impossible it was to please him no matter how well Jack and his younger brothers did at school, sport or anything. He couldn't remember a single compliment without a negative 'but' tacked on the end.

'I give her what she needs,' Hugo said. 'She goes to one of the most expensive schools in London. She's lacked nothing her entire life and yet—'

'You can't tell me one positive thing about her.'

Hugo tried to outstare Jack's steely courtroom gaze

but failed. 'I just want a divorce, damn it. That's what I'm paying you to do.'

Jack opened his drawer and took out a printout of the information he had received from the independent forensic accountant yesterday. He slapped it on the desk in front of Hugo Winters. 'I was surprised you could afford me until we did a little research. Want to explain why you want your wife and children to live with next to nothing while you have millions of pounds squirrelled away in offshore accounts in tax-free countries?'

Hugo's ruddy pallor faded and his bulk seemed to shrink in the chair as his shoulders dropped. He didn't bother reaching for the document Jack had put in front of him. He sat like a sulky youth caught out in some misdemeanour he didn't expect to be forced to take responsibility for.

'Here's the thing, Hugo,' Jack went on in the same firm don't-mess-with-me tone. 'You're going to have to find another lawyer because I no longer want to act for you. I can't represent a man who cares more about his money than his children's welfare.'

'But you have to act for me!' Hugo stood, a light of panic in his eyes. 'Everyone says you're the best.'

Jack rose from his own chair. 'I know what I'm good at and I don't need another win to prove it. This is a moral issue and I won't compromise myself by acting for you when I know it will harm your children in the long run.'

Hugo blew out his ruddy cheeks as if he was going to argue the point some more but Jack gave him a levelling look. 'One last word of advice. You need to love your kids more than you hate your ex.'

'I don't hate Edwina,' Hugo said. 'I'm bored and want a change. Marriage is hard work, especially when the kids are past the cute stage. Just wait until you're in my shoes.'

Jack was about to say he would never be in his client's shoes but then he thought of Sylvie. There was no way he would ever get bored with her. He was starting to realise why he was feeling so lonely. He was in love with her. The real deal love. The sort of love he wanted to have for the rest of his life. Why had it taken until now to realise it? All those years of squashing his feelings, pushing them down so deep inside him had made him unable to recognise what he was feeling in real time. He was feeling love, true and lasting love for the first time in his life and he couldn't wait to tell Sylvie.

But… Sylvie hadn't said anything about loving him. She had ended their fling because she felt compromised over the lawsuit. Well, that was already sorted because he was no longer Hugo Winters's lawyer. Could he take a risk and hope she felt the same way about him as he did her?

Sylvie was checking her emails while one of the hairdressers was styling her hair for her mother's wedding. She clicked on a work one even though she knew she should probably leave it until Monday. It was a message from her secretary informing her Hugo Winters had changed lawyers. Jack Wilde was no longer acting for him. Sylvie clicked off her phone and stared at her reflection in the mirror. Hugo had changed lawyers before, so it was crazy to think Jack might have walked away from the case because of her. Wasn't it? Because Jack Wilde was not the sort of lawyer to back down from a case he wanted to win. Was it because of the forensic accountant's report? It had come in on Thursday and she had skimmed through it but she had read enough to know it wouldn't serve Hugo well to persist in pretending he had no available assets for child maintenance.

'There, all done,' the hairdresser declared, stepping back with a smile, holding a large hand mirror behind Sylvie's head so she could see how her chestnut hair was styled in an elegant updo.

'It's lovely, thank you,' Sylvie said, smiling briefly, then vacating the chair for the flower girl.

Her mother came over to her and took both of her hands in hers. 'Darling, why are you frowning? Please tell me you're not having doubts about Patrick?'

Sylvie forced a smile. 'No, of course not. It's just a work thing.' She squeezed her mother's hands. 'You look beautiful.'

Linda blushed like a schoolgirl. 'So do you. It's a pity you didn't bring Jack but—'

'He wouldn't have come anyway,' Sylvie said. 'I ended our…fling.'

Her mother's eyes rounded to the size of dinner plates. 'Why? I thought you two suited each other so well. I was sure he was falling in love with you, and Patrick thought the same even though you told us you were just friendly neighbours. The way he looked at you all the time made me sure he was in love with you.'

Sylvie stretched her lips into a pained smile. 'That's because love is all you and Patrick can think about right now. Jack is a playboy.'

Linda began stroking Sylvie's hands with her thumbs, her gaze steady and serious. 'Did you tell him how you felt about him?'

'No, of course not.'

'Do you love him?'

Sylvie found it hard to hold her mother's searching gaze. 'I do but it's pointless because he doesn't want to settle down.'

'And you do?' There was a note of surprise in her mother's eyes.

'I didn't until I held Hamish, Natasha and Mariah's baby boy,' Sylvie said. 'I guess I was so frightened of falling in love after what happened between you and Dad that I locked away those yearnings and concentrated only on my career. But I realise now I want more than my successful career.'

'You want Jack.' Her mother said it softly, her expression full of love and concern.

Sylvie gave a tiny nod. 'But it's hopeless. And besides, I don't want to ruin your wedding day by talking about my stuff.' She forced a bright smile on her face and added, 'Let's have a glass of champagne to settle your nerves.'

'*My* nerves?' Linda laughed. 'I'm not nervous at all, just excited, but a glass of champagne sounds like a good idea.'

* * *

Sylvie had her phone on silent in her clutch purse but she heard it vibrating with a call. She ignored it but it rang three times. There were still a few minutes before the ceremony, so she took herself to a quiet corner of the garden and checked her recent calls. All three were from Edwina Winters. A flood of panic rushed through her and she wondered if something bad had happened to Mimi. She called back and within two rings Edwina answered. 'Sylvie? Oh my God, I can't believe it but guess what? Hugo has given me full custody and everything I wanted in the settlement. I'm sorry for calling on the weekend but I couldn't wait to tell you.'

Sylvie frowned. 'He did? Wow. But I heard he'd changed lawyers again.'

'He hasn't got a new one yet but he told me Jack had refused to act for him. I don't know what Jack said to him but he's agreed to everything I've asked for. When you next see Jack, will you please thank him for me?'

'I probably won't be seeing him outside of a courtroom but yes, I will.'

'But I thought you were—?'

'Neighbours, that's all,' Sylvie said, her heart pinching at the thought of being a witness to Jack's playboy lifestyle. She would have to move if it got too difficult.

Then she turned from the shady area under a grove of Japanese maples to see Jack Wilde striding towards her. He was dressed in a smart suit and tie and looked as handsome as ever, possibly more handsome than ever before. Her heart gave a jerk against her breastbone and her legs were frozen in place. 'Sorry, Edwina, I have to go. I'll call you Monday.'

'Okay bye.'

Sylvie put her phone in her purse with fingers that weren't quite steady. She snapped it closed just as Jack came to stand in front of her. 'Jack? What are you doing here? Did my mother invite you?'

'I'm being appallingly rude by turning up like this but I had to see you.' His expression was serious and he looked like he hadn't slept properly for weeks.

'Is Shadow okay?' Sylvie could think of no other reason for him coming to see her with such a grave look on his face.

A brief smile flickered on his lips. 'She's fine. She's moved in and taken up residence on my brand-new white sofa.'

Sylvie's eyes widened. 'Are you serious?'

He rolled his eyes. 'Talk about a pushover. All she wanted was smoked salmon and a few pats. Now we're best mates.'

'You and your legendary charm.'

He smiled at her. 'I'm hoping it's going to work right now.'

A butterfly flutter of soft wings brushed the floor of Sylvie's belly. 'Jack, why did you stop acting for Hugo Winters?'

'Lots of reasons but the main one is because he doesn't care about his kids. I would hate to be that sort of father in the future.'

Sylvie double blinked. 'But I thought you're not interested in being a father?'

He held her upturned gaze. 'I wasn't but then I met you.' He took her purse out of her hand and set it on the lawn at their feet. He straightened and took both of her hands in his. 'I think I fell in love with you when we first danced at the masked ball.'

Sylvie's mouth dropped open. 'You love me?'

He looked deeply into her eyes. 'I love you, Sylvie, and I beg you to put me out of my miserable loneliness and accept my proposal of marriage.'

Her heart leapt to her throat. 'Marriage?'

'I'm making such a hack job of this,' Jack said with a grin, drawing her closer. 'I love you with all my heart and soul. I love everything about you. I want to be with you and only you for the rest of my life. Will you marry me, my darling?'

Sylvie flung her arms around his waist and squeezed him as tightly as she could. 'Oh, Jack, I can't believe I'm hearing you correctly.' She leaned back to look up at his smiling face. 'I didn't realise I was falling in love with you but I think it might well have started when we danced at the ball.'

'You're the first person I've ever said those words to, my darling,' Jack said, his eyes suspiciously moist. 'I never told my parents I loved them and I've lived with that regret ever since. When they died, I locked down even further, burying my feelings, not even recognising them, much less allowing myself to feel them.' He squeezed her hands, his expression so tender and warm. 'It took me a while to realise why I was so agitated and restless after you called off our fling. I love, love, love you and will never stop saying it, even when we go through rough times as all couples do. Let's beat the divorce stats. Let's commit to being the happiest couple we can be.'

Sylvie nestled against him, feeling safe in a way she had never felt before. Jack was her rock, her anchor—and she was his. They were a team, ready and committed to fight whatever was thrown at them. 'I will always love you, Jack. I haven't said those words to anyone other than my mother since I was ten. It's also been hard for me to recognise what I felt because I too had taught myself to bury my true feelings. But I don't want to do that anymore, not now I have you by my side.'

Jack picked her up and swung her in a circle, then planted her back down on her feet and grinned down at her. 'This is the happiest moment of my life. I can't wait to get married to you. Do you mind waiting until my brother gets home? He's postponed his trip home again, but it shouldn't be much longer.'

Sylvie gazed up into his eyes. 'Of course I'll wait.'

Jack cupped her face in his hands, his eyes shining with love and tenderness. 'You are so beautiful inside and out. I know you're a career woman so I'm not insisting we have children but if we do, I know you'll be an excellent mother to them.'

'Do you want children?'

'I didn't until I met you and saw how protective and concerned you were about Edwina's kids and I realised you would be a wonderful mother.'

'Oh, Jack.' Sylvie stroked his lean, clean-shaven jaw. 'You have made me the happiest woman in the world.'

'Your mum might have something to say about that. I think the ceremony is about to start. Aren't you meant to be the bridesmaid?' Jack glanced at the assembled guests then back at Sylvie.

'Will you walk with me?'

'Now and always,' he said.

He bent down and picked up her clutch purse and tucked it under his arm. He took her hand and walked with her towards the guests. 'Do you think your mother and Patrick will forgive me for gatecrashing their wedding?'

Sylvie smiled up at him. 'Just use your legendary charm. It seems to get you exactly what you want every single time.'

Jack gave her a cheeky wink, his dimpled smile making her heart flutter. 'There's something I haven't done yet. Two things actually.' He stopped walking and turned her in his arms. He slipped his hand into his trouser pocket and took out a velvet ring box. It was a little faded but the name of the jeweller on the lid made Sylvie's eyes widen. He popped open the box and a beautiful cluster of diamonds glittered in the sunlight. 'As the eldest son, I inherited my mother's engagement ring. If you don't like it, we can have it redesigned.'

'Oh, Jack, it's so beautiful. I'd be honoured to wear it.'

He took the engagement ring out of the box and slid it onto her left hand. 'How about that? A perfect fit. It must be some sort of omen.'

Sylvie gazed at the ring on her finger, then looked

up at Jack again with a smile. 'What was the second thing you had to do?'

'This,' he said, and brought his mouth down to hers in a kiss that spoke of love and longing and the end of loneliness.

* * * * *

Were you blown away by Rivals' One-Night Rule*?*
Then make sure you check out the first instalment
in the Wilde Billionaire Brothers trilogy,
Fake Engagement Arrangement. *And why not*
explore these other stories from Melanie Milburne?

Cinderella's Invitation to Greece
Nine Months After That Night
Forbidden Until Their Snowbound Night
One Night in My Rival's Bed
Illicit Italian Nights

Available now!